RETURNING TO SHORE

RETURNING

TO

SHORE

CORINNE DEMAS

Carolrhoda LAB
MINNEAPOLIS

Carolrhoda Lab™
An imprint of Carolrhoda Books
A division of Lerner Publishing Group, Inc.
241 First Avenue North
Minneapolis, MN 55401 U.S.A.

**For reading levels and more information, look up this
title at www.lernerbooks.com**

Cover and interior photographs: © Trigger Image/Alamy (shoreline cover and
title pages); © iStockphoto.com/spet (sand texture); © Raphael Christinat/
Shutterstock.com (shoreline front and back matter).

Main body text set in Janson Text LT Std 11/18.
Typeface provided by Linotype AG.

Library of Congress Cataloging-in-Publication Data

Demas, Corinne.
    Returning to shore / Corinne Demas.
        pages   cm
    Summary: When her mother remarries again, high schooler Clare has
no choice but to spend time with her biological father, Richard, at his home
on Cape Cod, where she begins to understand him and learn that she may
have been wrong about a lot of things.
    ISBN 978–1–4677–1328–3 (trade hard cover : alk. paper)
    ISBN 978–1–4677–2403–6 (eBook)
    [1. Fathers and daughters—Fiction. 2. Diamondback terrapin—Fiction.
3. Turtles—Fiction. 4. Remarriage—Fiction. 5. Cape Cod (Mass.)—
Fiction.] I. Title.
PZ7.D39145Ret 2014
[Fic]—dc23   2013018618

Manufactured in the United States of America
1 – SB – 12/31/13

FOR AUSTIN AND GARY

1

The white balloons were released from behind the privet hedge at the exact moment that Clare's mother kissed her new husband. Clare watched the balloons rise. They were snatched by an errant wind and blown stage left, free now, and undisciplined. Clare kept her eyes on the balloons until they were out of the scene entirely. Then she turned her eyes back on the small platform where her mother and Tertio, as Clare called Ian, her mother's husband number three, beamed out at the invited guests.

"I hope this one lasts longer than the last one," said Eva, Clare's aunt, who was seated at her left. Eva was a short, overweight woman, and she was taking up more than her allotted space on her white folding chair. Clare shifted a little so she wouldn't feel the pressure of Eva's silk-clad hip next to hers.

Clare hadn't wanted to think about Peter, but it was impossible not to.

"Hey, you'll always be my girl, no matter what," he had said. But now he was living with someone and Clare didn't see him very often. It was she who had told Peter about Tertio, when she'd met him for lunch a few months before. They were sitting in one of the booths by the windows, in the café where Peter worked on his novel.

"I'm happy for Vera," said Peter.

"How can you say that?" she had asked him. "I thought you loved her!"

"I did love her," said Peter, and Clare had noted the past tense, "but it didn't work out. What can I tell you? People have to move on with their lives."

"That's a pile of shit," Clare had said, and though Peter's eyebrows expressed his surprise he didn't say anything, just shrugged.

Tertio was a decade older than Vera, two decades

older than Peter. His grown children were seated at the main table with Clare at the reception. Vera had wanted to have Clare and them stand on the platform during the ceremony, but Tertio's daughter had refused, so the idea was scrapped. Clare had been relieved. The daughter was an artist who worked with aluminum, and she was wearing a dress that was cut low in back to reveal an elaborate tattoo that must have hurt like hell when it was done. She kept ducking out to smoke. Tertio's son was tall and bony and was in college someplace. He didn't talk at all, and Clare wasn't sure if he was a snob or just painfully shy. Eva was doing her best to try to bring him out, with no results whatsoever. Tertio kept gazing at Vera with stupid rapture and did not notice the shortcomings of either of his children. Vera looked more relieved than enraptured, but then again she was not a woman who was given to rapture. Even at the triumphant conclusion of a case she had litigated for weeks on end, she expressed little more than a touch of satisfaction.

Clare's dress was a flower print that Vera had picked out at Lord & Taylor that looked like it was designed for a ten-year-old. It had a little matching jacket that Clare didn't wear, even though her arms were chilly. Vera had actually selected three dresses and let Clare choose, but the other two were even worse. Vera had taken Clare with her to the hairdresser's in the morning and Clare's hair had been done up in a chignon. When Clare got home and caught a glimpse of herself in her bedroom mirror, the hairdo looked like it belonged on someone else's head. She'd pulled out the hairpins and shaken her hair free so she looked like herself again. When Vera had seen her she'd given one of her dramatic sighs. Vera had dark, luxurious hair that looked good no matter how she wore it. It was the one thing Clare wished she'd inherited from her mother; her own hair was wispy and a color that even her friends called "dirty blonde."

When the many courses of dinner were finally over, Vera and Tertio cut the wedding cake, and waiters scurried around delivering a slice to every guest. The wedding cake was extravagant, buttercream, that had cost hundreds of dollars. Clare hadn't felt like eating any of it and had left her piece on her plate.

"You have to take that with you," said Eva. "You put some under your pillow tonight, and the man you dream of will be the man you marry."

Right. Buttercream mushed under her pillow. And whom did she have to dream of? There weren't any boys she knew that she could imagine growing up into someone she might want to marry. Besides she wasn't planning on ever getting married. Her mother had been married three times now. Clare had been the flower girl at the wedding to Peter, a beautiful wedding in a meadow beside a river, with all the guests barefoot and people playing guitars and everyone singing . . . and look what became of that.

***

After the reception Clare went upstairs in the inn with her mother to change and get her things for her trip.

"Everything was just perfect, wasn't it?" said Vera, as she hugged Clare.

"Sure Mom, it was great."

Vera laughed a little and put her hands on Clare's shoulders. "To tell you the truth the salmon wasn't quite warm enough. And the champagne wasn't quite cold enough."

"I'm sure you're the only one who noticed."

"Ian noticed the champagne. He didn't say anything, but I could tell."

"Ian didn't notice anything but you, Mom."

Vera smiled. "You may be right, darling." She caught a glimpse of herself in the mirror. "I never liked the color peach before, but I think it was just right. I think the dress worked out. What do you think, sweetheart?"

"I already told you, Mom, the dress is fine. You looked—" Clare hesitated for a moment; words spun through her head: beautiful, glamorous, elegant . . . "Divine," she said. It was her wedding gift to her mother.

Vera threw her arms around Clare again. "Oh my darling," she said, "I am so happy. I am so very, very happy." She let go of Clare slowly, then immediately burst into action, laying out her clothes for the trip. Clare's suitcase and backpack were already in the trunk of Eva's car. Vera helped Clare with the back zipper on her dress and folded it expertly while Clare put on her jeans and T-shirt.

"I still don't see why I can't stay with friends while you are away," she said. "Molly said I could stay at her house, and Susannah invited me to go to Colorado with her."

Vera turned quickly to look at her. She didn't say anything, just tilted her head, a 30-degree angle of disappointment.

Clare sighed. "I know, I know," she said, "we've been over this a hundred times. Even so, Mom . . ."

"Who knows?" said Vera, after a pause, "you might actually have a good time—well, even if not a good time, at least an interesting time. You might discover something you two have in common."

"Mom, I haven't seen him since I was a baby."

"Three," said Vera. "You were three."

"Three, then," said Clare. "And I don't remember a thing about him."

"You'll learn about him, then. And he'll learn about you." She smiled, and Clare had a sudden urge to smack her, smack that smile. But it was Vera's wedding day, and you couldn't smack someone on her wedding day, not to mention the fact that that someone was your mother.

"OK," said Vera, and she shoved Clare's duffel bag to the side and sat down on the edge of the bed. "I know this isn't easy, darling. None of it. But he does have some rights in the matter, and this was such a perfect opportunity." She took Clare's hand and pulled her to sit beside her. "It's only three weeks. I'll be back before you know it." She kissed the side of Clare's face, and though Clare didn't intend to, had no expectation that she would do this, she buried her face against Vera's arm and cried, quietly, but cried all the same.

If Vera had asked her why she was crying, she would have said, "I miss Peter. If you and he were still together none of this would have happened."

But Vera did not ask.

2

Eva and Clare were on their way soon after the string quartet had packed up their instruments and gone off to their next gig. The musicians were four Juilliard students, and they seemed rather shrill and giddy when they left. Clare wasn't sure if it was the champagne, which they had started enjoying at the beginning of the Mozart, or if it was because Tertio had tipped them so generously (Clare had seen the hundred-dollar bills). Tertio's daughter had left long before, and his son had fallen asleep on a sofa in the lounge, a thin line of spittle dragging down the corner of his mouth.

Vera and Tertio saw Eva and Clare off, though the

newlyweds turned to go back inside the inn before Eva finished turning the car around. Clare caught a last glimpse. They had their arms linked behind their backs, the way skaters might as they circle the ice rink.

"Well," said Eva cheerfully, as she pulled out onto the main road, "that's done. How are you feeling?"

"OK, I guess," said Clare.

"I was trying to figure out what to get your mother for a wedding present," said Eva, "and of course there was nothing she didn't have. And then she suggested this." Eva took her eyes off the road longer than she should have and looked at Clare. "Not that I'm sorry to have a chance to spend a little time alone with you. This is fun for me. Though I hate driving, and I don't do bridges."

"How are we going to get to Cape Cod, then?" Clare asked.

"Your father is going to meet us in the rest area along the canal on this side," Eva said. "Don't worry, we have it all arranged."

When Eva said "we" Clare knew she meant Vera, for Vera was a champion of organization, and Eva, by her own admission, was not. It hadn't always been like this. Clare could remember a time when her mother was as casual about things as her younger sister. But Vera had become fiercely organized around the time she decided to reinvent herself: going back to law school, moving into the city, chucking Peter.

"I have to be," she had told Eva, "it's the only way to get anything accomplished." Now she divided up her day into ten-minute segments. "Billable" minutes, she had pointed out. Every ten minutes counted, was worth money. Where back when she was married to Peter time went by all on its own, unaccounted for. Ten minutes spilled into the next ten minutes and nobody kept track of it. Sometimes Clare missed the school bus in the morning because Vera had been oblivious about the time.

"I'm so sorry, darling," Vera would cry out, in anguish, "I promise I won't let it happen again." But it did happen. Not that Clare minded. When she missed the bus Peter would drive her to school—sometimes in Vera's car, sometimes on the back of his motorcycle.

"I can't believe I ever let you do that," said Vera recently, when the subject of riding motorcycles had come up. "I must have been out of my mind."

Time was different for Clare, too, back then. In her old elementary school everything was relaxed and she could take as long as she wanted to finish a project or the book she was reading. Now everything was scheduled from the moment she got up in the morning. At school, bells clanged at the end of every class period, and the only time she could talk with her friends was during the 45 minutes they had for lunch. She used a purple pen to mark things on her calendar, because it looked softer than red, but the calendar was still filled up. And when school was finally out this year, all of her free time had been swallowed up by preparations for her mother's wedding.

The inn where the wedding had taken place was deep in the countryside—or so it had seemed to Clare—but the highway was only ten minutes away. It was a newly widened section of road, with embankments still raw and in some sections a lurid green, where a mixture of grass seed and tinted fertilizer had been spread. When Vera had selected the place for the wedding she had liked the convenience to the highway, but had made sure, when she stood outside with Clare, that you couldn't hear the distant traffic.

"I should never have had that last cup of coffee," said Eva. "I'm going to have to pee as soon as we get to the first rest stop. How are you doing?" she asked.

"I'm fine," said Clare.

"I thought I should drink coffee since I'm going to be driving half the night, but there's always a price to pay."

"Are you driving all the way back to the city after you drop me off?" asked Clare.

"No way!" said Eva. "I'm heading on to Boston, staying with friends." Eva had friends all over the place. All over the world, in fact. "If you have friends to crash with," she'd once advised Clare, "you'll never have to spend money on a hotel."

"You said half the night," said Clare.

Eva laughed and poked Clare with her elbow. "You are such a literalist," she said.

Clare dug in her pocket and pulled out a hair elastic. She leaned forwards in her seat and gathered her hair into a ponytail and secured the elastic around it. There was still a residue of whatever hair product Vera's beautician had used that morning. She'd wash her hair as soon as she could. There would certainly be a shower at this place she was going to. Wouldn't there be?

"What did you think of the wedding?" Eva asked after a while.

"I don't know," said Clare, and shrugged. "What was I supposed to think of it?"

"You were watching the balloons floating away during the ceremony, and from the expression on your face it looked like you wanted to grab onto them and make your escape."

Clare was surprised by this. She hadn't been aware that Eva had noticed her at all during the ceremony, and she hadn't been aware that her face had shown anything at all.

"I just feel bad about Peter," she said. "That's all."

"If you love Peter—and who wouldn't love Peter?" said Eva, "—you'll be happy for him that your mother finally pushed him out of the house and moved on to someone else. He and Vera were a disaster together. I'm just surprised they lasted as long as they did."

"A disaster?" asked Clare.

"He was fine as a lover," said Eva, "but as a husband . . . ?" She turned to look at Clare. "I'm sorry, honey, am I telling you something you never heard before? What did Vera say to you about the reason she dumped Peter?"

"She said he wasn't serious enough, he lacked 'gravitas,' " said Clare.

Eva laughed so hard she had to blot tears from her eyes. She dug in her pocket and extracted a well-used tissue to blow her nose before she spoke again. "I'm not laughing at you," she told Clare, "I'm just laughing at—oh God, I can just hear Vera saying that, 'gravitas'! Well, she acquired plenty of gravitas herself, I guess. And then she acquired Ian."

The thought of Ian made them both silent for a while.

"Look at it this way," said Eva. "He's dull, but he's solid. He's rich. He's smart. And he loves your mother. I'd say that's about as good as you could hope for."

"I miss Peter," said Clare, and she closed her eyes and pressed her cheek against the cold glass of the window.

"Yup," said, Eva, and she reached across and gave Clare a one-armed hug.

"I wish I could have stayed with him now. I know he's living with someone, and he and Mom aren't exactly talking to each other, but still . . ."

"You can understand how Vera wouldn't want to be dealing with Peter at this time."

"She could have let me stay with my friends, then. She didn't have to ship me off this way."

"She's not exactly shipping you off," said Eva. "She's sending you to visit your father. He's been wanting to see you for years. And this—well, this worked out."

"He's been wanting to see me for years?"

"You didn't know that?" asked Eva.

"Not really," said Clare.

"Well, I didn't think it was any big secret. I thought you talked to him on the phone."

"On Christmas. He calls every Christmas. But we don't really talk. He asks me what I'm doing in school and I tell him. That's about it."

"He supports you," said Eva. "You knew that, didn't you?"

"I guess."

"Pays your tuition at snooty-tooty academy, pays for your oboe lessons, your tennis camp, your ortho-dontist, your computer, your clothes, your food. Until Ian came along he paid for a lot of Vera's stuff, too. You can't say he hasn't been generous all these years."

The word "generous" was not one Clare had ever heard used about her father. It made him seem more like a real person. Vera rarely talked about him much, and if she ever did, the adjective she relied on was "smart." Clare had always assumed that the checks he sent were simply a legal obligation, not that he'd had a choice about any of it.

"Do you hate him, too?" asked Clare.

"Hate him? Nobody hates him!" said Eva.

"Mom does."

Eva shook her head furiously. "She thought she did, once, but that was long ago."

"Does he hate her?"

"You'll have to ask him that," said Eva.

"He did move to the other side of the whole country."

Eva actually seemed to think about her answer before she spoke. "He didn't do that to get away from her," she said. "From what I understood, he wanted to be out in Silicon Valley, where things were happening in his field. And she didn't want to move. That's when marriages often fall apart," said Eva. "One spouse wants to move and the other doesn't."

Clare could easily imagine her mother saying, "I don't want to move." When Vera said something, she stuck to it. Still, that didn't explain *him*.

"He never came back to visit, not even once," said Clare.

"California does that to people," said Eva. "It sucks them in and frazzles their brains, and they never make it back to the right coast again."

Clare turned in her seat so she could look at Eva straight on. "So how come he came back now?"

"I have no idea," said Eva. "And I don't think Vera does, either. All I know is that he took some kind of early retirement and decided to move back to Cape Cod, where he owned a house, and got himself involved with something to do with reptiles."

"Reptiles?"

"Reptiles, amphibians. One of those things, thank God, that we don't have in New York City." Eva took her hands off the steering wheel and waggled them in the air for emphasis.

"How come he owns a house on Cape Cod?" asked Clare.

"It was his parents' place. He inherited it, and I guess he decided to hold on to it. I don't know what it is exactly. A house, a cottage. A tent."

"And this is where I'm going to be stuck for three weeks?"

"It looks like it," said Eva. "I'm sorry, honey. I offered to put you up, but Vera thought this visit was important. If you get desperate, give me a ring and I'll come bail you out. And besides, look on the bright side, you wouldn't want to be stuck for three weeks with Vera and Ian in his villa in the south of France."

"I don't think it's a villa," said Clare. "I think it's just a house."

"House, schmouse," said Eva.

She turned her attention back to the road, and Clare tilted her seat back and closed her eyes. She didn't think she'd fall asleep, but she must have, because when she opened them again it was early evening, and they were pulling off the roadway into a rest area.

The parking area was long and narrow, and ran parallel to the road along the water. There were cars and campers parked in slots along the length of it, but it wasn't full. Eva drove slowly towards the end. In the last space Clare saw an old Volvo station wagon. There was a man outside the car, leaning back against the car door. He was waiting for someone. He was waiting for her.

3

Eva pulled in next to the waiting car, but she didn't turn off the engine right away. There was a bike path along the Cape Cod Canal, and a family of five came riding past them, on the sidewalk by the parking area. The youngest kid was straggling in the back, weaving along on a bike that was too big for him. "Wait for me!" he cried out to the bikers in front of him. "Wait for me!"

Eva sat in the car until they had all biked passed. She flicked at the key chain that dangled from the key in the ignition, let it swing back and forth a few times, then she shut off the engine. The man next to the station wagon stood up straight, but he didn't move any closer to them.

Eva took in her breath. "Well here we go," she said, and she opened her car door and stepped outside. Clare waited for a second, then she stepped outside, too. It was breezy outside. Inside the car she'd had no awareness of the wind, and the smell of the canal—a dense aroma of seaweed and salt water—was as much a surprise as if she had stepped out into a foreign country. She walked around the front of the car, towards Eva. And towards this man who was her father.

She knew him from photographs. But they were all photographs of someone much younger. This man was grey haired, with a small beard, and he was older—not as old as Tertio, perhaps, but old enough so the man in the photographs might have been his son. He was taller than Tertio, but probably not as tall as Peter. He was wearing shorts and a work shirt with a pocket that held several pencils and pens. He looked as if he had been called away in the middle of some project. He certainly had not gotten dressed up to meet her.

"Hello, Clare," he said. He began to hold out his hand, but seemed to think better of it and let it drop by his side. His voice sounded like the voice she recognized from their phone calls, but he didn't look like anything she had expected. She realized she'd never really tried to picture him. He'd always been just a voice.

"Hello," she said. What did he think, now, seeing her?

The three of them stood awkwardly for a moment until Eva recovered her usual gregariousness. Like an actress who had momentarily forgotten her lines she brightened and spoke in a voice that was unnecessarily loud.

"It's been a long time, Richard," she said. "You're looking good. You're looking really good."

"You're looking good, too," said Richard, and he allowed Eva to seize his hand and shake it vigorously. It didn't seem as if he was a shy man, so much as a man who wasn't inclined to acquiesce to expected formalities. Clare feared there would be another long interlude of silence, but Eva was quicker this time.

"I hope we didn't keep you waiting here too long," she said. "We hit some traffic around New London."

Traffic? Clare didn't recall any, but perhaps it was while she asleep. Or maybe they had spent too much time at the rest stop. Or maybe Eva was just saying this because they had just left later than they should have.

"Not a bad place to wait," said Richard. Which implied that he had waited, had been kept waiting.

"So, I hear that you decided to opt out of the corporate crazy world and take up the pleasures of early retirement."

"I made some changes in my life, yes," said Richard. "How's it all treating you?"

"Me?" said Eva. She shrugged. It seemed to Clare that Eva was genuinely uncertain whether to attempt a real answer, or whether the question was mere politeness. "Well, since I've seen you last I've had about a dozen different jobs—one of the jobs actually twice—I mean I left and did some freelance work, then came back to it." Eva's voice trailed off. Richard was looking at her still, but Clare guessed Eva could tell he wasn't really listening.

"Did you end up marrying that man who was a graduate student in . . . ?" Richard asked. "Sorry I can't remember what field he was in."

"No reason you should have," said Eva. "I barely remember myself. And the answer to your question is no. I didn't marry him. Or anyone else either, in spite of my sister's best efforts."

"How *is* Vera?" asked Richard.

"Oh Vera is—" She looked at Clare now. "Help me out here," she said.

Clare didn't know what to say. Didn't know what was wanted of her.

"What a question!" cried Eva, saving Clare from saying something inane. "Sorry, honey." She turned to Richard. "Vera has just married a supportive, stable, mature male. I think she's fine."

"I'm glad," said Richard, and he said it in a way that sounded as if he actually meant it.

Clare was relieved that the conversation seemed finally to be over and Eva headed to the car to open the trunk. Richard came with her and took Clare's suitcase and duffel bag, and carried them over to his car. He lifted the hatch door and pushed aside a pile of buckets and nets to make room for Clare's things. Clare wedged her backpack next to her suitcase.

Eva extracted an index card from her bag and starting handing it to Richard. "Vera's contact information and Clare's emergency health information," she said.

"Does she think I'm five?" Clare asked.

"I won't be needing that," Richard said. "I'll take good care of her." He smiled at Clare. It was the first smile he gave her.

"Of course you will," said Eva. "But please take the card anyway, just so I can tell Vera I carried out her orders."

Richard tucked the card behind the pencils and pens in his shirt pocket.

"If anything comes up that might require the assistance of an aunt, just give a holler," said Eva.

Richard nodded and opened the passenger door of the car. There was nothing for Clare to do but get in. Eva got something out of her car, then placed a small shopping bag on the seat behind Clare. "The piece of cake," she said. "Don't forget to put it under your pillow. I'll be wanting a full report of that dream." She leaned down to kiss Clare good-bye.

Too quickly, she was off.

4

They didn't speak at all until they had crossed over the Cape Cod Canal. The bridge was the kind of high bridge that's arched so there's a moment when you can't yet see the opposite side and you wonder if you're just heading off into space. In the far distance, off to the left, Clare could see the bay. The dark blue of the canal below was pockmarked with white waves. The boats were toy-sized, and the bicycle path was a dark ribbon, stretched along the shore. Clare thought of the boy on the bike.

"Wait for me!" he had cried. "Wait for me!" Had they waited? Surely they had waited.

"We're taking route 6A, not the highway," said Richard, after they had gotten off the bridge. "Any time I go off Cape, I always take the scenic route back, because then I feel I'm really here. On the highway, you could be anywhere." He concentrated on his driving for a moment, then, when they came to a stop at an intersection he turned to her again.

"It's about an hour to the house from here. Would you like to stop somewhere before then?"

Clare wondered if he meant to ask if she needed to use a bathroom, but was actually embarrassed to say so. "I'm fine," she said.

"Did you want to get some dinner?"

"Oh no, I had a late lunch. I've had a lot."

"That's right," said Richard. "I imagine you would have."

They rode most of the rest of the way in silence. Clare kept thinking he would start talking again, but he didn't. Some people didn't like to talk while they drove, Clare knew, but that certainly wasn't the case with her mother, who used car trips as an opportunity to lecture her. And it wasn't the case with Eva, who had talked the whole way. Clare fingered her iPod on her lap, but she felt shy, somehow, putting her earbuds in. She had the feeling that her father might think it rude. Now and then she stole a glance at him. He was handsomer in profile than full face. She had thought his hair was grey, but it wasn't entirely. It was bleached out, dull blond, and real grey only in places. Wispy hair, like hers. His face and arms were tanned, and there was a white mark on his wrist, the ghost of where he had worn a watch. Clare wished now that she had asked Eva more about him. She wished she had asked her mother more about him, too.

What did she know about him? Very little. On her birthdays he sent her cards that said, "Now you are ___" for whatever age she was, and inside he'd Scotch-tape some money. When she was younger it was a ten-dollar bill, later a twenty. Last year it had been a fifty. He taped it carefully so that most of the tape was on the card, and only a little of it on the money, and so she could peel it away easily. She looked at his hands on the steering wheel now. His fingers were callused, the nails cracked. It was hard to imagine those rough hands selecting a birthday card, taping the money inside it.

What else did she know? At one time, he'd started a collection of first edition books, which he'd left behind with Vera when he moved to California. The books weren't those nice leather volumes—the kind that look expensive—they were just plain books with their paper jackets in plastic sleeves, but when Vera had sold them, they'd been worth a lot.

She knew that when Vera had wanted him to give up his rights to her and let her be adopted by Peter, he hadn't let that happen. Vera had wanted her to have Peter's last name, Giancelli, "a name that sings," Vera had said, but he hadn't let that happen, either. Vera had taken on Giancelli herself, but when she'd gone back to law school she'd gone back to her maiden name. Now, in an act of uncharacteristic docility, she'd submitted herself to Ian's last name, Ruderman, a name that did not sing. A name, Clare thought, that anyone would have changed to something pleasanter a long time ago.

If she'd been allowed to take Peter's last name, Clare felt, she'd be able to be connected to him always. She'd be his real daughter, instead of the daughter of this man, whom she was sitting next to in this old station wagon. This station wagon that smelled like . . .

Clare tried to think of what it was. The Cape Cod Canal? They weren't that close anymore, but it smelled as if they were.

"It would be nice if we could get back before dark," said Richard, suddenly. "It's always something to come to the bridge and look out over the marsh."

"I thought we already crossed the bridge," said Clare.

"We crossed the Canal bridge. This is the bridge to the island. It's a small bridge, wooden."

Clare thought he'd continue talking, but he didn't. Eventually they turned off the main road onto a road that headed towards the bay, a road that got narrower and winding. They emerged from the woods, and the paved road ended. Richard stopped the car and turned off the engine.

Clare looked at her father. He gave her a smile, and then gazed ahead, his hand outstretched, as if he was offering the view to her. In front of them was a marsh—a huge, flat, open space, that went on and on. The sun had just set and the sky was that trembling, soft pink before evening turns into night. It was absolutely quiet, as if sound itself did not exist. They sat there for a while, looking at the still marsh, and Clare let herself sink into the quiet. I'll remember this, she thought. I'll remember this quiet and the way this looks, this enormous marsh, and the sky at dusk. I'll use this sometime in a story. The first job of a writer, Peter had told her, was to be an observer. And she was training herself to do that. Not just observing things, but finding a way to translate them into words in her head, storing them up to use later. That's what Peter did, for the stories he wrote, for the novel he was working on. It was reassuring now to be thinking of a story, to imagine herself as a character in a story, instead of just herself, a girl in this bare, open place, with a man who was her father, but a man whom she didn't know at all.

After a few minutes Richard started up the engine again. "Time to cross the Blackfish Island Bridge," he said.

The bridge was, in fact, wooden, and it was just wide enough for one car. They drove up one side, across a creek, then down to the marsh on the other side. The car's tires thumped on each plank.

"What if someone's coming the other way?" Clare asked.

"Doesn't happen too often," said Richard. "And if it does, one car waits on the side till the other's crossed over. No need to worry. No cars in sight."

"I wasn't worried," said Clare. "I just wondered."

"Unless, of course, it's one of those washashores, in one of those monster houses on the dunes, tearing over this bridge in their SUV."

"What's a washashore?" asked Clare.

"It's what they call newcomers, around here."

"I guess I'm a washashore," said Clare.

"You? Not you, Clare. You're third—no, fourth-generation Blackfish Island. It's your great-grandparents who built the original cottage out here."

"But I've never been here before."

To her surprise, Richard stopped the car, stopped the car right where they were on the sand road, in the midst of the darkening marsh. He turned to her.

"What made you think that?" he asked.

Clare shrugged. "I don't know," she said. She felt a little frightened. Not that he was angry, but that it seemed as if he might become angry.

"You came here every summer, when you were little," said Richard. "Vera didn't like it out here, so we came for only a week or two. But you were certainly here." Now he sounded more sad than angry.

He started up the car again and continued driving. The road was so rutted Clare grabbed onto the seat to steady herself for the bumps. It didn't seem as if they were on a real road, just a worn path through the marsh grass.

If she'd been here before, how come she didn't remember it at all? Shouldn't there have been some click of recognition, something that seemed familiar, even if it was something she'd experienced when she was young, even before she had words. But everything was strange, this place, this man who was her father.

Her best friend, Susannah, had a father who lived in Colorado, and Susannah visited him every summer. She was there now, would be there until the middle of August.

"It's nice that you get to see him every year," Clare had once said.

"You call once a year nice?" Susannah had asked. "I think it sucks big time."

"Well, I never see my father," said Clare. "I haven't seen him in, like, eleven years." Susannah shut up for the moment. "Well that's something," she finally said.

Later, when Susannah had heard about Clare's proposed visit, she was surprised Clare didn't want to go.

"I don't even know him," Clare had said.

"Aren't you curious?" Susannah had asked. "I mean, this guy's your father. You have his genes."

"That doesn't mean I'll like him."

"You don't like your mother," reasoned Susannah, "but aren't you glad you've at least had an opportunity to get to know her?"

You couldn't argue with logic like that.

5

The house was on one end of the island, nestled among the pines. There was a light on outside, by the door, where squadrons of insects had met their demise. The door was unlocked. Richard stepped in and flipped on the light in the kitchen, then started carrying Clare's stuff in from the car.

Once the car had been emptied they stood awkwardly for a moment in the kitchen.

"Would you like something to eat now? Something to drink?"

"I'm OK," said Clare. "I just need to call my

mother. I'm supposed to call and let her know I arrived safely."

"The phone's right there," said Richard, pointing to a table in the corner.

"That's OK, I've got my cell."

"No reception out here," said Richard. "Closer to the bridge, sometimes you can get something, but right here, we seem to be out of range."

Clare called on the kitchen phone, and Richard left the room, as if he thought she might want to have privacy. But he needn't have; Vera wasn't answering. Clare got her bright voice-mail message. It ended with "*ciao*"—a leftover from her life with Peter.

"I'm here, Mom," said Clare. "I made it." She waited for a moment, then she added quickly. "Have a good time." Then she hung up the phone. She waited for Richard to return.

"Guess I should show you around," he said.

The house was a small cottage that had been expanded over time, wings added in two directions. The kitchen, Richard explained, was the original structure. Walls had been taken down to make one large room out of three. All that was left from the old living room was the fireplace. Beyond the kitchen was a bedroom filled with boxes.

"Stuff from California," Richard said. "This house was completely furnished—it's been rented out all these years—so I didn't need to unpack much."

On the other side of the kitchen there was a living room with a high ceiling. One wall was a bookcase, two stories high, entirely filled with books.

"My mother, your grandmother, was a high-school English teacher," said Richard. "She loved books. She had all her literature alphabetized by author," he said. He went over to a shelf and tilted his head to read the titles. "This is all Henry James," he said, pointing down the length of the shelf. "Have you read anything by James?"

"*The Turn of the Screw*," said Clare. "I had to read it for school." She felt lucky she had been able to answer so quickly. She'd had to write a paper about it; that's why she remembered it. The paper was all about point of view, how you couldn't trust the narrator, how her version of things was just the way she presented them, not necessarily the way things really were. If Richard had asked her more about it, Clare could have said some "insightful" (her teacher's comment at the end of the paper) things about Henry James, but he didn't ask. She was a little disappointed. She wanted her father to think she was smart. She didn't know why it mattered, but it did.

In the other downstairs bedroom there was a desk and a big table, both covered by papers and computer equipment. There were piles of papers and books on the file cabinets. There was a single bed in the corner, and a chest of drawers. That had a pile of papers on it, too.

"Terrapin Central," said Richard.

"What's terrapin?" Clare asked.

"It's what I study," said Richard. "The Northern diamondback terrapin."

Clare shrugged.

"Here, let me show you something," Richard said, his voice was suddenly filled with excitement. He turned to his computer and brought up an image on the screen. It was a big turtle. Someone was holding it up for the camera, with two hands, and the turtle looked angry to have its picture taken.

"*Malaclemys terrapin*, a threatened species, the wonderful, elusive turtle of the salt marsh. Isn't she a beauty?" asked Richard. At first Clare thought he was kidding, but then she realized he wasn't. He was staring at the turtle as if he really thought so.

"Number 986. A recapture. Found early this morning." He shuffled among his papers on the desk and pulled up some sheets stapled together. He put on reading glasses and scrutinized the print. "Female, 1,448 grams. Some marginal scarring along the right carapace. First observed 20th of June, 2011."

He stopped talking, took off his glasses, and looked up at Clare. She hadn't noticed his eyes before, and now she saw that they were brown. Vera had blue eyes, and her own eyes were a hazelish-greenish that her friend Susannah had insisted she call "green." A mix of her parents' eye color—or maybe her eyes were entirely her own. She had tried to seem interested in what Richard was saying, but she hadn't really been following him. She was wondering, instead, where she was going to sleep. Certainly not here, but it didn't seem possible that all those boxes could be moved from the other bedroom.

Richard seemed to have read her thoughts. "Well, enough of this for the moment. Let me show you upstairs," he said. "I cleaned out the bedroom up there; I thought it was nicer than the one in back. You can get a glimpse of the marsh."

Clare hadn't realized there was an upstairs, but there was. It was built into the peak of the roof, one-half of the living room's open ceiling. It was a small bedroom, with a tiny bathroom and closet. The ceiling sloped, and the bed and bureau were built in. It felt like a cabin on a ship.

"I'll bring your things up," said Richard. "You look around. See what else you might need."

In the bathroom, towels had been laid out on the edge of the sink. The bathroom smelled of lavender— the source, a cake of soap still in its paper wrapper in the soap dish.

In the bedroom, the bed had been made up. The quilt still had a price tag on it. Clare guessed that it had been purchased for her visit. On the wicker table by the window there was a vase with some roses in it. So he had planned for her coming, had gone out of the way to make things nice for her. She wouldn't have guessed he was the kind of man who would think to cut roses, put them in a vase. But he had.

Richard brought her bags up the stairs in two trips.

"I'm going out now to make my rounds, checking to see if there are any new nests—it's terrapin nesting season. Might be an hour or so. You can come with me if you like, or maybe you'd rather stay here. Unpack. You must be tired. It's been a long day."

Clare nodded. "I guess I'll stay."

"Did you want me to make some dinner? Do you want to have something to eat before you go to bed?"

"No, thanks, but I'm not really hungry," said Clare. "I think I'll just go to bed."

"If I'm not back before then, good night," said Richard. "I'll see you in the morning."

"Good night," said Clare. He closed the door behind him as he left the room. She sat down on the foot of the bed. She heard him walk down the stairs, and not soon afterwards she heard the screen door snap behind him. He didn't urge her to eat something for dinner; he didn't ask her if she needed help with anything. She couldn't believe he'd just go off and leave her alone in this strange house, but he had. He'd just gone off to do whatever he did with those turtles, as if she hadn't just arrived.

She got up slowly and began to unpack. She arranged her clothes in the drawers and hung her two summer dresses in the closet. She emptied her backpack and stacked her books on the bureau. She'd been using a postcard from Susannah as a bookmark, a picture of a cute bear cub in a tree, and she took it out and wedged it in the corner of the mirror. She felt suddenly hungry, but when she opened the bedroom door and looked down the stairs the house seemed dark and unfamiliar, and she didn't want to walk all the way to the empty kitchen. In the little shopping bag Eva had given her was a plastic container with the piece of wedding cake. Clare ate it now. It was a huge piece of cake, sweet and buttery, with a hint of almond. She ate it all, and she licked the icing that had smeared along the plastic lid. She knew she would feel sick later, but she didn't care.

She went to the window and looked out. She could smell the marsh, a bit like the smell of the sea, but denser, sadder. She couldn't see much of anything— just a few frail lights, far in the distance. There was the sound of the first stirrings of wind, a rustle in the marsh grass. What did her mother imagine things were going to be like? Did her mother imagine her father would just leave her on her own in a house in the middle of a dark nowhere, the first night she got there?

And what had she imagined? In fact she hadn't had the space to imagine anything at all before now. Her mind had been full thinking about her mother marrying Tertio, and thinking about Peter, the fact that it would now be impossible that he and her mother would ever be together again. But during the car ride out here she had hoped that her father's silence was just the way he was when he drove, and once they got to the house he'd be different, more conversational, more interested in her. She'd hoped that they would stay up late talking, getting to know each other. That he would explain why he'd been out of her life for so long, and why he'd decided to turn up in her life now. That he'd say, "Clare, I'm so glad we have a chance to be together, at last."

Right.

For the first time ever, she felt angry at Peter. If only he hadn't been so . . . what was it, unwilling? unable? to be just a little bit more of what her mother wanted him to be. Then maybe Vera wouldn't have wanted to "move on" (her words) from him. And they could have been together, as they were in the years before, the three of them, happy. The way families were supposed to be.

6

Clare awakened to sunlight pushing into the room and a smell—the smell of the marsh—that seemed at first to be part of her dreams. She had kicked off the quilt sometime during the night and she pulled it back up over her shoulders and closed her eyes, but she didn't fall back asleep. The combination of the smell, which filled not just her lungs, but her whole body, and the feel of the sun, warming one side of her face, was hauntingly familiar. She opened her eyes and let the room come into focus: her stack of books on the bureau, the postcard she'd tucked into the mirror frame, the vase of roses on the table by the window.

She closed her eyes again. There was something she remembered from when she was very little . . . it was morning, and she was blinking in the sunlight and smelling the marsh. Yes, the marsh. So she did have a memory of Blackfish Island. She *had* been here. She got up and went to the window. The house was on a hillside that sloped down towards the marsh. If her father cut down the trees—pitch pine and scrub oak— there'd be an expansive view of the marsh and part of the bay. But if anyone had ever cleared the trees, that had been long ago, and they'd been left to grow up again. All she got now were little sections of the view, little pieces of distance.

When Clare went downstairs she found a note for her on the kitchen counter. It said, "Help yourself to breakfast. I'll be back shortly."

It was unsigned. They hadn't yet faced the issue of what she should call her father, and so she had done her best to avoid calling him anything at all. "Dad" sounded fake, somehow, but "Richard"—she'd never heard him referred to as Rich or Dick—sounded odd, too. It was easy for him; there wasn't much else to call her except Clare.

The handwriting was small and surprisingly even, as if he had drawn a pencil line to guide him. She'd read an article once about telling personality from penmanship, but all she remembered was that if the letters leaned backwards that meant the person was somewhat shady. Or was it insecure? These letters were all straight up.

Richard came back in just as she was pouring milk on her cereal. He didn't say good morning; he just asked, "Everything OK there?" nodding at her breakfast.

"It's fine," she said. "It's exactly what I eat."

He smiled a little. "I can't take any credit for that, I'm afraid. Your mother sent me a list of your food requirements. I just made a trip in to the supermarket and bought what she listed: orange juice without pulp, two percent milk, French vanilla frozen yogurt, veggie burgers, green seedless grapes." He pointed at a large fruit bowl. There were about eight bunches of grapes; they spilled out of the bowl.

"That's a lot of grapes," said Clare, feeling unpleasantly like a small child.

"She said you liked grapes." He made himself a cup of coffee and came and sat across from her at the counter. He stirred his coffee, took small sips. He looked like he had something to say to her, but he didn't know how to begin. When she finished her cereal she carried the bowl over to the sink.

"Want me to put this in the dishwasher?" she asked.

"I haven't used the dishwasher yet," he said.

"You haven't?"

"Just one of me. Easy enough to wash what I use. But I suppose with you here now it might be worth trying."

Clare opened the dishwasher door and was about to put her bowl in, when she realized it was full of paper products.

"I've been using it as storage," Richard said. "Let's just pile stuff up here and I'll figure out another place for it later." He started to hand things up to Clare, and she set them on the counter. They stood close beside each other, but only once did his arm brush against hers. They worked efficiently, as if the passing of paper towel rolls and boxes of paper napkins from his hands to hers had been choreographed in advance. Clare noticed how similar their hands were—the same shape, the same curve of their thumbs. Vera had long slender hands, an octave and a note, but Clare's hands were squarer, her fingers shorter—she could barely reach an octave. Even though her father's hands were bigger and his nails were rough, her hands had been formed from the same mold. It had never occurred to Clare before that hands could reveal a connection between them, that hands could matter that way.

Soon the dishwasher was empty, and the counter was stacked with rolls of paper towels, paper napkins, paper plates. Richard reached for the cereal bowl and set it in on the top rack of the dishwasher.

"Why don't we give this thing a test run now," he said. "It worked for the last tenants, but it's been a while." He put in detergent and started up the dishwasher. There wasn't anything to watch, but they both stood there, looking at the dishwasher, listening to the water rushing in, invisible behind the white door. Clare wondered if they would continue standing there for the entire cycle.

"I guess it works," said Richard, finally. "I'm going out now to finish my rounds of the island. Do you want to come with me?"

"I guess so," said Clare.

"Your mother instructed me to remind you to put on sunscreen," said Richard. "If you don't have any, there's some in the bathroom."

"Oh, I have plenty," said Clare. "She packed me enough to last the next three summers."

"I'm not surprised," said Richard. He smiled, but only slightly.

"Are we going to be going swimming?" asked Clare.

"It's low tide now," said Richard. He sounded as if she should know this. "No swimming. But if you want to go this afternoon, I could show you where people swim."

Clare wondered if that meant he expected her to go off swimming on her own. She couldn't imagine Vera would be very happy about that.

"OK," she said.

There was a path that ran from the house down to the marsh. Clare followed behind Richard. It wasn't a path anyone had designed, it was just a sandy, worn path. At Tertio's house in the country—now Vera's house, too—all the paths were part of the landscaping design. They were carpeted with wood chips, freshly applied on a regular basis by the landscaping service. Nobody ever made a path just by going someplace.

***

The tide was so low it was hard to imagine the sea had ever covered what now looked like part of the land. You could tell where it had been, though, because it had left behind a band of seaweed when it had receded. Richard walked quickly, and seemed to expect Clare to keep up. Far out in the marsh Clare saw the arched wooden bridge. It seemed to connect nothing with nothing. When they came around the bay side of the island Richard slowed his pace. There were boats at anchor, lying on their sides. They looked sad somehow, like beached whales dying on the flats. Richard was scanning the beach in both directions.

"Are you looking for something?" Clare asked.

Richard stopped and turned to her. For a moment she wondered if he had forgotten she was there.

"Terrapin tracks," he said. "This is the season when the females come up on shore to deposit their eggs. I'm trying to locate the nests, and put a cage over each one to protect it from predators: foxes, skunks, coyotes."

Clare kept her eyes on him while he spoke and tried to think of a question to show she was interested. "Do you catch the turtle in the cage?" she asked.

Richard smiled, as if he'd never thought of this possibility before. "No, the turtle just lays her eggs, buries them in the sand. Then she goes back to the sea. The eggs are on their own."

"If the eggs are buried, how do the foxes know they're there?" asked Clare.

"They've got great noses," said Richard, and he tapped his own, which was long and sunburned.

"What happens when the eggs hatch? How does the mother turtle get back to the babies if they're all in a cage?"

"Good question," said Richard, and Clare brightened. It wasn't like she was really interested in the turtles—after all, they were just turtles—but she wanted Richard to feel she was interested. She wanted him to talk with her. "Once the female terrapin has laid the eggs, she's done," said Richard. "She returns to the bay. When the eggs hatch in September, the hatchlings have to make their way on their own up over the dune, and to the marsh."

"And the male turtles?"

"They never come up on shore at all. Their part is done once they've fertilized the eggs."

If she knew him better, Clare might have asked if that's the way it had been with him. But as soon as she thought of it for a minute, she knew, she would not have been able to say anything. It was too weird. God—just thinking about it now made her so embarrassed she could not even look at him. But if he had made any connection in his mind to the subject, he didn't let on. He had started walking again. There were big houses along the dunes. They were set up high for the view, and had long, wooden stairways down to the beach.

Richard noticed her looking at them. "People build those monstrosities too close to the edge of the dune, and then—then," he repeated, his voice rising, "they want to build a revetment."

"What's a revetment?"

"A wall to keep the dune from eroding. The problem is, it destroys the natural geologic progression; dunes were meant to erode. If you put up a wall, the sea steals the sand from somewhere else." Richard shook his head. "Those people. They want to put in lawns.

Terrapins can't nest in lawns. They drive their SUVs at top speed along the dirt roads. They don't see a terrapin, let alone a hatchling." He took in his breath and let it out slowly, as if he had practiced this breathing technique. "You see what I'm up against, Clare?" he asked. He sounded resigned now, tired out.

"I guess," said Clare, but he wasn't really looking at her. He was already walking fast down the beach. He was looking intently at the sand in front of him. Once again, he seemed to have forgotten she was there.

They had gone three-quarters of the way around the island, past the houses on the dunes, when they came across the tracks. They didn't look like much of anything to Clare—she would have walked right over them if she was on her own, but Richard spotted them from a distance and sprinted towards them.

"Here we are," he said. He was excited now. He bent close to the ground, like a dog sniffing a trail, and scrambled up towards the dunes. Then he sank to his knees, dug around a bit, and sat back.

"Too late," he said evenly.

Clare came up beside him.

"This is what a predated nest looks like," he said.

There wasn't much to see. A few scraps of leathery-looking shell.

"That's what happens when you go away," said Richard. He stood up slowly, brushing the sand from his hands. "With a species so fragile like this, every nest counts, every egg counts."

Clare could feel her eyes filling up, and she turned her face away from him. He'd probably think it was the turtles she was crying about.

But he didn't. "I'm sorry, Clare," he said. "I'm not blaming you. I'm blaming myself."

She turned to him quickly. She didn't care if he saw her crying now. "Maybe you shouldn't have left them, then," she said.

He stared at her.

She'd blurted that out quickly and there was no going back now. "Just so you know," she said, "I didn't want to come here this summer. It was you who asked for me to come."

She started running back to the house. Either she was faster than he was, or he didn't try to catch up with her. She ran into the kitchen and up to the room which was her room and closed the door behind her.

7

It was half an hour later when she heard him coming upstairs. He knocked on the door.

"You can come in," she said. She was sitting on the bed, leaning against the wall. Her knees were bent and she had her arms wrapped around her legs, holding them close against her body.

He stood in the doorway. "I'm not very good about talking about things, Clare," he said. "Never have been. But I guess as much as I don't like talking, I've got to say something now."

He leaned sideways against the doorframe, ran his finger up along the grain of the wood. "Looks to me that we've got two choices here. Either we can throw in the towel and call up your Aunt Eva and you spend the rest of the time with her. Or we hang on and see if we can get anything going for us."

Clare didn't say anything right away. She looked down at the quilt, studied the pattern.

"I'd say either way was OK with me," said Richard, "but that wouldn't be the truth, Clare. The truth is that I'd rather you said you wanted to hang on, because that's what I'd like to do. Give us some more time. See what we can do? Or maybe I should put that differently." He paused for a moment, cleared his throat. "What I should say is, give me more time, see what I can do. What you're doing is—well—OK."

"All right, then," said Clare.

"All right, what?"

"Number two," she said, and she looked up at him now.

Richard stood straight up. "That's good," he said. "Thank you, Clare." And he went back downstairs.

8

In the afternoon Richard said they would go kayaking, so Clare went upstairs to put on her bathing suit. She'd brought three, and none of them seemed right. She had to stand on the bed to see all of her in the mirror over the bureau. Finally she chose the one that covered her the most, and pulled a big T-shirt over it.

Down at the beach there was a pile of small boats along the side of low dunes.

"Have you kayaked before?" Richard asked.

Clare shook her head. "Then I suppose we should take a little time to get you used to it before we head out netting."

Richard hoisted a small boat up and carried it down to the water. It was the smallest and ugliest boat in the group. It was a dull orange, and looked as if it been battered by rocks. "This is my baby," said Richard, and he gave it a tap with his foot.

The words jolted Clare. "This is my baby," Vera had said, the first time she introduced Tertio to Clare.

The other boat Richard carried down, to Clare's relief, was a larger, newer one. It was bright red. When he set it on the sand next to his boat, his boat looked even smaller and rougher.

"I got this one for you to use," said Richard. He said this casually, but looked back at her in a way that made Clare guess he was hoping she would be pleased. She wasn't sure if he had borrowed the boat for her to use, or if he had actually bought it. Either way, he had thought about her, planned something for her visit.

"Thank you. I love red," was all she could manage to say.

He had outfitted her with a life jacket. Fortunately it wasn't one of those awful orange kinds that you wore like a sausage around your neck, but a vest with a zipper up the front. She stood by the kayak now, holding the paddle he had given her.

"Tell me what kind of experience you've had with boats," said Richard.

"I use the rowboat on Tertio's pond," said Clare. Richard's eyebrows rose before she could catch her slip.

"Mom's new husband's pond," she corrected herself.

Richard was smiling now.

"His name is actually Ian," said Clare.

"I know," said Richard. "So he has a pond, does he?"

"Only a very small pond," said Clare. She didn't want him to have the wrong impression.

"A swimming hole?" asked Richard.

"Well, it's kind of mucky, so you don't swim in it. You swim in the pool." She had made things, she realized, even worse.

But Richard just smiled. "Don't worry, Clare, it's fine with me that your mother married a millionaire. I'm happy for her. I want her to be comfortable."

A millionaire? That sounded so . . . Well, perhaps he was. That wasn't what was wrong with Tertio, though. It was his personality. It was the way he was. Sure, he had a pond, but did he ever do more than glance at it in the distance? All he ever did outside was swim a few laps in the pool on weekends, then lie on his lounge chair and make calls to his office, while Vera lay on her lounge chair beside him, reading the Sunday paper. If Clare said, "I'm going off to explore the pond," Vera would look up from her page and say, "That's nice dear." Once, just to test her, Clare had said, "I'm going off to drown in the pond." Tertio had just grunted, but Vera never missed anything.

"What did you say?" she asked.

"I was just kidding, Mom."

And Vera had given her a look which conveyed exactly what she thought of Clare's joke, then gone back to her reading.

**

Before they got into the kayaks, Richard gave her a paddling demonstration on land. She looked quickly in both directions, but even though there was no one else on the beach she felt embarrassed standing there paddling in the air. He stood behind her, put his arms around her and placed his hands beside hers, on the paddle. This was the closest he'd been to her. She looked at her hands right next to his, the hands she had inherited, distinct as a face. Their hands dipped right, left; right, left.

Once they got out on the water, the kayak felt tipsy. Richard had her lean far to each side to show how far it would go without flipping, but even though the water was only waist deep, she felt nervous.

"You'll get the hang of it soon enough," said Richard. "Compared to rowing, it's a pleasure. For one thing, you're looking in the direction you're headed, for another thing, your center of gravity is nice and low."

It *was* nice to be low in the water, almost as if she were sitting right in the bay itself. Richard had her paddle around in circles and showed her how to turn and how to back up. It wasn't that hard. As she paddled with Richard across the inlet she grew more confident. The kayak did tip as she leaned to each side, but it easily righted itself. The water was calm and she was surprised by how quickly they made it to the beach on the opposite shore. Richard helped her out of the kayak and pulled it up on the sand beside his. She looked back where they had come from. The boathouse on the shore was farther in the distance than she had imagined; it could have been a toy.

"Tired?" Richard asked.

"Not really," she said.

"Clare, you're a natural," said Richard, and she felt a flush of pride. No one had ever said this to her before. Certainly not the tennis instructor at Tertio's club. "Clare, I'm afraid you're not a natural," he told her, "but with some practice there's no reason why you can't have a backhand, too."

"Before we go out netting," said Richard, "I'd like to do some work on emergency techniques. These boats don't easily capsize, but just in case, I want you to know how to handle it."

Clare's heart started beating fiercely. All the sense of mastery she'd been feeling dropped entirely away. She got back into her kayak and followed Richard out to where the water was just over her head.

"You're a decent swimmer, aren't you?" asked Richard.

Clare nodded.

"And you have a life jacket on, so you'll bob right up to the surface, right?"

Clare nodded again.

"If you're a strong kayaker, and it flips upside down, you can right it yourself. Here, I'll show you," said Richard. He paddled out a distance from her, flipped the boat so it was upside down, then somehow—she couldn't see how he managed—he got himself out of the kayak, swam up beside it, and then flipped it upright again. His hair and beard were soaking wet now and his face looked thinner.

"If you find yourself upside down in the water, you just swim out and under and come up on the side of the kayak. The kayak won't sink; no need to worry about that. You hang onto the side until you catch your breath, then you right the kayak and climb back in again. That's the tricky part." He heaved himself up onto the kayak and he looked somewhat ridiculous as he worked to get his legs up and squeeze himself into the little boat. He was breathing hard, and he seemed vulnerable for a moment, a way Clare hadn't seen him before. Once he was seated, he looked like himself again.

"Ready to give it a try?" he asked her.

"OK," said Clare.

"Come out here."

She paddled out into the deeper water. The sunlight illuminated the top several inches of water, but didn't reach farther into the dark blue-green below. She tried tilting the boat far to one side, but each time, just before it got dangerously close to tipping over, she panicked and righted it quickly.

"You've got to try it just once," said Richard.

"I can't," she said.

"You can," said Richard.

She paddled around again and tried leaning, but once again, her instinct made her pull herself upright. Except this time the boat didn't respond. In an instant she was upside down in the water, clambering to find the surface. She thought she was drowning. She banged against the side of the boat, clutched at something hard, and suddenly found she had broken through the surface of water to the sweet air. She grabbed onto the side of the boat and gasped for breath. Then she saw her father's face.

"You did that, didn't you?" she asked.

He nodded.

"You didn't have to do that," she cried.

"I did," he said.

Clare worked for half an hour to get herself back into her kayak. When Richard had demonstrated the technique, it had looked hard, but when she tried it, with him coaching her from his kayak, it seemed impossible. She had barely enough strength to hoist her body up onto the hull of the boat and every time she did, she slipped back into the water or pulled the kayak upside down on top of herself. It didn't make things easier that she'd started laughing. And once she started laughing, Richard had started laughing, too.

"I need to take a rest," she said, and she leaned her head on the kayak and closed her eyes and felt the pleasant rhythm of the boat beneath her cheek moving up and down with the waves that she, herself, had made. When she opened her eyes she saw that Richard was leaning his head back in his kayak, eyes shut, with his feet up outside of the hull. He looked as if he was dozing. Quietly, she slid down into the water and swam up to his boat. Then she grabbed the side of it and pulled it over. The kayak tipped on its side and all in a second Richard was dumped out of the boat. He came up spluttering. He grabbed onto the overturned kayak and shook his head, like a wet dog.

For an instant the look of astonishment on his face frightened her—she didn't know him well enough to tell if he might be angry or not. She wondered what had possessed her to do a thing like that. What had she been thinking? But then he smiled at her—it was a smile that was full of pleasure and surprise, a smile that was different than any he had given her before.

"I guess we're even now," he said.

9

They'd decided that the turtle netting would wait until the next day. Richard had suggested they spend some time at the house, then go out for pizza for dinner. It was, Clare realized, what he considered something special, something he thought she'd like. With Vera, pizza was a meal of last resort. It wasn't something you ever planned on; it was what you had when meetings ran late and no one had the time to cook. The years when Vera was in law school, it was too often pizza for dinner. But Clare would not have wanted Richard to know this. He had obviously gone to the trouble to find out where to get pizza, since he said he never ate pizza himself.

Clare settled on the deck to read one of the paperbacks she had brought with her while Richard went to his study to work on his turtle website. It was not a book from Peter's list—those were all books that she read to impress Peter—no, this was a novel that Susannah had passed along to her, a book that Vera would say had no intellectual value, but still it was fun. And she felt she deserved something fun after braving the water of Cape Cod Bay.

The deck was on the back of the house, facing the view. Once it must have been a place you could sit and enjoy a broad view; now, she positioned her chair so she could see a slice of the water. The chairs were old-fashioned, wood, slung with canvas so faded the orange and green stripes were barely visible. When she'd first unfolded her chair, pine needles had coughed up on the deck.

Clare hadn't heard a car drive up—there was no driveway, just a sand road and a walk from the drive-way to the house. But then she heard voices. A woman's voice said, "Oh, I'm sorry, Rich, I wouldn't have just dropped over if I knew you had a guest here."

Rich?

And Richard said, "It's my daughter."

Clare turned around. His daughter. It was the first time he'd said that word.

The woman was blonde and slender. "Oh, your daughter!" she said, with evident surprise. "I didn't know—"

"She's here visiting for a few weeks," said Richard.

"Let me say hello," said the woman, and she pushed open the screen slider and came out on the deck. Richard followed her. Clare instinctively put the book facedown on the deck beside her chair. If she was going to be meeting someone, she didn't want them to be thinking of her as the kind of girl who read junky YA novels—of course she *was* reading a junky YA novel, but still, it was just because it was summer. Clare pulled herself out of her chair. She felt small sitting in the low chair, like a kid.

It occurred to Clare that Richard might not have introduced them—either because he was the kind of man who didn't think to do such things, or because, for some reason, he wasn't eager for them to meet. But the woman had clearly wanted to meet Clare. She had a sheaf of papers in her hand, which she gave to Richard, and stepped up to Clare now, hand extended. She was older up close than she had looked at a distance, a woman who had once been quite pretty and was, Clare thought, used to thinking of herself that way, though her teeth were too big.

"I'm Steffi," she said.

"I'm Clare."

Richard stood a bit behind them. Steffi turned to him. "You never told me you had a daughter," she said. He shrugged. She leaned towards Clare confidentially. "Your father is a man of many secrets," she said in a teasing way, but there was also a note of criticism.

It's true, thought Clare, a man of many secrets. There was an awkward moment, a moment when it was Richard's turn to say something. But he didn't. He just stood there, not extending himself to help the conversation. But if Steffi was disappointed by his lack of social grace, his inhospitality, she didn't let on.

"I work with Rich on the terrapin project," she said, her voice cheerful and excited. "On *his* terrapin project, I should say. He's our guiding light."

"Hardly," said Richard dryly.

"You know how modest he is," said Steffi to Clare.

Clare nodded as if she knew, but she didn't know at all. "The project was his idea; he got the grant money; he organized the volunteer network—I'm just a volunteer; I'm not a real naturalist.

"I'm not trained as a naturalist, either," protested Richard.

Steffi ignored him. "And when journalists want to do a story about the project, he won't take any credit for what he's doing."

There was another long pause. At this moment Clare would have expected Richard to offer Steffi something to drink—but he didn't. They all stood there, and Steffi smiled brightly at Clare. She was remarkably resilient. Perhaps she was so familiar with his awkwardness she didn't take it personally.

"So, you'll be helping out with the turtles while you're here, I bet."

"I guess so," said Clare.

"That's great," said Steffi. "Nesting season, you know, is the busy time; we can use all the help we can get. Have you done this before?"

Clare shook her head.

"But you've been to the island before?"

"Oh, yes," said Clare. "Of course." She stole a look at Richard, and he caught her eye. His mouth moved slightly, not quite a smile, and he gave just the slightly hint of a nod.

Again there was a pause. Steffi took in her breath, pulled up her shoulders. "I've got to be going," she said, "great meeting you, Clare. We'll be seeing each other, no doubt." She turned towards Richard and touched his elbow. Her three fingers rested for a second on the fabric of his blue work shirt, then pressed cloth against skin. "I have some cages in the car I could use your help with," she said. Her flip-flops slapped against the soles of her feet as she walked off. Clare felt a touch of —what was it? jealousy? and on whose behalf? Steffi was the kind of woman who would have irritated Vera, a woman who seemed as if she hadn't put a lot of work into looking attractive, but who was attractive anyway. But it wasn't Vera whom she was feeling for; it was herself, for the fact that this woman seemed to know her father better than she did. Clare sat down and opened her book. She didn't want them to think she was watching them to see how they dealt with each other when they weren't with her. She didn't know what was between them. It seemed clear that Steffi was interested in her father—but was he interested in Steffi?

When he came back to the deck, he said, "Ready to go for pizza now?" Nothing about the visit from Steffi. So she didn't bring it up, either.

10

It felt strange to Clare to be going up and over the wooden bridge, leaving the island behind. Out on the main road Blackfish Island seemed as if it was a continent away. People speeding along to other parts of the Cape would never know that it existed, perhaps would not know that a place like it *could* exist.

The restaurant was noisy with big ceiling fans that swirled the air around but didn't do much to cool it. The teenagers who were working there looked sweaty and tired. Still, Clare envied them. It would be fun to have a real summer job, to be working with a bunch of friends and get to wear one of those red shirts that said

"Dave's Crew" across the back and had a name tag on the front. You probably had to be at least sixteen to get a job like that, though.

Richard studied the menu. "Should we get a whole pizza each or share one?" he asked.

"Aren't they kind of big?"

Richard caught the attention of the girl behind the counter. "How large are the pizzas?" he asked.

The girl's name was Maureen. Her dark hair was held up on her head with a plastic clip as big as a lobster claw, but half of the curls had escaped, and she kept pushing them off her damp face with the back of her arm.

"Regular size has eight slices. It would feed a family of four if you each had two pieces."

"Or a family of two, if you each had four?" asked Richard.

Maureen looked puzzled. "I guess," she said.

"In that case," said Richard to Clare, "I think we should share a pizza. Are you a traditionalist? Or do you want to try some exotic toppings?"

"You can get it half and half," suggested Maureen.

"A workable solution," said Richard. "Ready to

order?" he asked Clare. She nodded. "I'll have mushrooms and extra cheese."

"And I'll risk the clams and pesto."

They found a table near the side window that looked out on a miniature golf course. It had a lighthouse and a windmill that were so detailed you could imagine that they were real, just far in the distance. Clare watched a family that had little twin daughters who kept pushing each other to get ahead. Behind them, an older brother was taking his shots very seriously.

"Interested in playing?" Richard asked her.

Clare shook her head. "No, that's OK," she said.

"That's a relief," said Richard. Clare was glad she hadn't said she wanted to play. If she had, he probably would have done it just to please her.

When their number was called, Richard got up and claimed their order. He placed the plates carefully on their table and slid back onto his seat.

"You might want to check for a souvenir of Maureen's tresses before you take a bite," he said. Clare couldn't tell from the expression on his face whether he was teasing her or not. It was like that comment about the miniature golf. He might have been joking, but she couldn't be sure.

The pizza wasn't especially good, but Richard didn't seem to notice. "I haven't had pizza in years," he told Clare.

"They have pizza in California, don't they?"

"They do. They have every imaginable configuration of the species, but I think the last time I had pizza it was nothing fancy, at a place near campus where your mother and I liked to go."

Clare, with a piece of pizza half dangling from her mouth, looked up at him suddenly. This man, with the sun-bleached grey hair and the frayed work shirt, who was sitting across the table from her, had dated Vera. Had actually been married to her.

"You seem surprised," said Richard. "I guess Vera eats only gourmet pizza these days."

"She doesn't really eat pizza much anymore," said Clare. "She used to eat it a lot. Sometimes Peter made it for dinner, from scratch."

Richard's face was down, looking at his plate.

"Peter, Vera's second husband," added Clare.

"I know Peter," said Richard.

"You do?" asked Clare, brightly. "I didn't know you knew him."

Richard looked up at her slowly. "Peter was on the scene before I moved to California."

"Oh," said Clare. "I thought Vera met him in a workshop she was taking after you had moved away."

"Workshop, yes," said Richard. This time he was looking straight at Clare, waiting for her next question. But what could she ask?

"Don't worry, Clare," he continued. "Peter's not to blame for the end of your parents' marriage. And he was a good stepfather to you, wasn't he?"

Clare wanted to say something about Richard's use of the past tense. Peter was still her stepfather, wasn't he, even if he and Vera weren't married? But she felt that Peter was not a subject that Richard was eager to talk about.

"Sure," she said. It seemed unfair to Peter not to say something more on his behalf, not to say how wonderful he is.

"How about some ice cream for dessert?" asked Richard. "I noticed a place on the way here."

"OK," she said.

There was a long line at the ice cream place, and Clare was afraid Richard regretted suggesting they stop.

"I don't really need ice cream," she said.

"No one needs ice cream," said Richard, and he took his place stoically in line. When they got their ice cream they got back in the car and Richard handed his cone to Clare while he started up the engine. When they were out on the main road again she handed it back to him. Her ice cream was soft-serve, and she had to work fast with her tongue to keep up with the drips down the sides of the cone.

By the time they had turned off onto the smaller road that led to the Blackfish Island Bridge, Richard had popped the last two inches of his cone into his mouth and wiped his hand on his shirt front, and Clare had reduced the swirls of vanilla to a mound barely higher than her cone. Somewhere, beyond the trees, the sun was setting now, and the sky was the faint violet color of dusk. There was a boy on a bicycle riding towards them. He was on an old-fashioned bike with big handlebars, and he was riding in lazy loops. He didn't have a helmet on, and he was barefoot. Richard slowed way down, but a car came up behind them—a jeep—and passed them just as the road curved to the left. The driver spotted the bicycle rider just in time, honked and swerved to miss him. Richard slammed on his brakes. The jeep raced off. The boy managed to keep his balance on the bike. He looked back over his shoulder at the jeep, then continued on his way. Richard drove a little farther, then pulled to the side of the road. Clare had gripped her ice cream, and her finger had poked through the cone to the cold inside. She started to lean over to take a big lick of the cone, but something made her turn to look at Richard before her tongue met the ice cream. He was bent over, his head on the steering wheel.

"Dad?" she asked. "Dad, are you all right?"

He lifted his head slowly. He was breathing heavily, as if he had been running. She dropped the ice cream cone to the floor of the car.

"What's the matter?" she asked.

"I've got to get out of the car," he said. "I've got to get some air."

"Dad! What should I do?"

He flung open the door of the car and scrambled

outside. But once he was on his feet he gripped the side of the car with one hand, his other clutched his chest. His breath came in small spurts.

"Are you having a heart attack?" she cried. "Should I go for help?" There were no other people around that she could see, but there was a mailbox just ahead of them at the end of a driveway, and there must be a house there not far away.

Richard held on to the door frame and leaned in the window. "I'm all right, Clare. It's not a heart attack. Don't worry. I'll be all right." He opened the car door and lowered himself cautiously to his seat. He was breathing more evenly now, as if he had practiced this, as if he was making himself slow down.

"What can I do?" asked Clare.

"Can you drive?" asked Richard.

"I don't have a license," said Clare, "but I've driven a little."

"Can you drive a stick shift?"

"No," said Clare.

"We'll just sit here for a moment, then," said Richard. "Just give me a moment to catch my breath."

Richard sat still with his eyes shut. Clare watched

the sky begin to darken, the colors fading until, eventually, there were no colors at all. She thought about the ice cream on the floor of the car and wondered if she should do something to clean it up, but ended up just moving her feet back. She closed her eyes and listened to the traffic in the distance. A pickup truck came along the road towards them, and she opened her eyes. The truck slowed for a moment when it passed them, then kept on going. Its headlights opened a swath of the darkness and grew dimmer, until it was too far away to see. Somewhere in the woods a night bird began a monotonous, plaintive call.

Finally, Richard opened his eyes. "I'm all right now. I'm ready to get back home."

"What happened to you?" Clare asked.

"I had a panic attack," said Richard.

"Not a heart attack?"

"Nothing to do with my heart. My heart is sound as they come. It's what happens in some situations—"

"You mean because of that car that went by?"

"The kid on the bicycle," said Richard. "I was afraid he was going to be hit."

"He wasn't hit," said Clare.

"I know," said Richard. "But there was a mo-ment—" He put the car into gear and pulled out onto the road. They drove up and over the Blackfish Island Bridge, the planks thumping under their weight. The smell of the marsh was familiar and comforting to Clare.

Richard didn't say anything until they were back at the house.

"I'm sorry that I frightened you, Clare," he said.

"That's OK," she said. "How are you feeling?"

"I'm fine now," said Richard. "Nothing to worry about. I owe you more of an explanation. Maybe to-morrow. In the meantime, believe me, I'm fine." Rich-ard gave her a slow, sad smile. "Good night, Clare," he said.

She'd called him Dad before. She cried it out then without thinking, but now she felt self-conscious about saying it.

"Good night," she said.

11

In the morning Richard was gone when she woke up. There was a note on the kitchen counter telling her he'd be back by nine. Clare was eating breakfast out on the deck when the phone rang. She ran to get it only because she thought it might be Richard—otherwise she would have felt shy answering the phone in his house.

"Aunt Eva!" she cried.

"Hi baby, how are you doing?" Eva's voice was distant and crackly.

"Fine."

"Reception's lousy so I better talk quickly," said Eva. "I'm going up to visit some friends in Maine. If you want, I can come and pick you up first. Are you ready to bail out?"

"No, I'm OK." She said it quickly, before she thought about it.

"If I'm in Maine I'll be about six hours away," said Eva. "I don't want you to be stuck there."

She thought for a moment now, but her answer was the same. "I'm not stuck. It's fine."

"You're sure?"

"I'm sure." Clare paused a beat or two. "Eva?"

"Yes?"

"Did Vera meet Peter while she was still married to Richard?"

There was a pause at the other end of the phone. Clare thought maybe she'd lost the connection, but then Eva let out a whistle.

"Wow. Let me guess. Vera gave you a prettied up version of the story and Richard is telling you something else."

"Sort of."

"Well, honey, the truth is that Vera and Peter discovered each other while Vera and Richard were still married. But if you ask me if it hadn't been Peter it would have been someone else. She and Richard weren't exactly a match made in heaven. When Richard got the job in California she wouldn't have gone to be with him, even if Peter wasn't in the picture."

"I'm starting to have trouble hearing you," said Clare.

"Any other bombshell questions you'd like to ask before I lose reception completely?"

Clare thought about what happened the night before. There was a lot to ask about that. But it wasn't just the poor connection that made her hesitate. It seemed like a private thing that had happened with Richard, and even though Eva was someone she'd always felt she could tell everything to, this seemed like something that Richard wouldn't want Eva to know.

"No," she said. "Have fun in Maine."

"Thanks, baby. Have fun out there on Goldfish Island. Call me if you need me, and even if it is six hours away, I'll come running. I love you!"

"I love you, too," said Clare but by that time Eva's connection was gone.

It was still only eight o'clock. Clare finished her breakfast and put her dishes in the dishwasher. The house seemed very quiet. Clare wandered into the living room and looked at the books on the bookcase. One whole section was nonfiction, books about nature and geology. There were lots of books about marine biology. Clare pulled out a fat book that said *Seaweed* on the spine, but it was just line drawings and lots of dull text. It was hard enough imagining someone devoting his life to writing about turtles—they at least had behavior you could observe—but seaweed!

The door to Richard's bedroom was open. Clare stood in the doorway and looked in. If Richard hadn't wanted her to enter the room surely he would have kept the door closed. Still, she entered cautiously, checking over her shoulder to make sure Richard wasn't home yet. The room was crammed with stuff, but strangely it revealed little of the man who inhabited it. It was all about work. It spoke only of Richard's preoccupation with terrapins, but little of the man himself. The only personal items visible were a wooden hair brush on the dresser that was missing a few clumps of bristles and a wadded up paisley handkerchief. Clare longed to open the dresser drawers and look through them, but that seemed like a tremendous breach of privacy.

If Richard were to arrive suddenly and discover her in his bedroom that would be awkward enough. But if he found her looking through his drawers that would be impossible to explain.

On the bedside table a pair of glasses held a book open. She guessed they were reading glasses since she hadn't seen Richard wearing them. She lifted the glasses and held them up to her face. If she looked through Richard's glasses would she have a sense of the way her father saw the world? But the glasses made the room out of focus. She held up the book, *The Collected Poems of W.B. Yeats*, but the poet was unfamiliar to Clare. The letters were magnified, louder. She looked at the poem that the book had been opened to: "The Wild Swans at Coole." She read the poem through and lingered on the last two stanzas.

Unwearied still, lover by lover,
They paddle in the cold
Companionable streams or climb the air;
Their hearts have not grown old;
Passion or conquest, wander where they will,
Attend upon them still.

But now they drift on the still water,
Mysterious, beautiful;
Among what rushes will they build,
By what lake's edge or pool
Delight men's eyes when I awake some day
To find they have flown away?

It seemed even more private, perhaps, to see what someone had been reading in bed at night than to be snooping through their dresser drawers. Clare wondered if Richard would be embarrassed to have her know he read poetry—poetry certainly seemed to make him seem more vulnerable than, for instance, a book on seaweed. But she guessed not. Richard seemed like the kind of man who just did what he wanted to do and felt no apologies for it.

Clare laid the book back on the table and placed the glasses exactly as she had found them. She went to the doorway again and listened for the sound of Richard coming home, but the house was as still as if she were the only person who had ever lived there.

Clare went over to Richard's desk and sat down.

The desk was a wooden door set on filing cabinets. There was a hole where the doorknob had once been. The desk chair had worn-out armrests and squealed when Clare swiveled. Peter had had a fancy desk chair that Vera had complained cost too much money.

"It's ergonomic," Peter had explained. "It's important to have something proper to sit on when you're writing. The mind works better."

"My creative genius!" Vera had said, laughing, and she kissed Peter full on the lips. That was back when Vera had loved Peter and believed in his talent. Later, she'd gotten impatient with him. While she was in the library studying for the bar exam, she resented that he'd take his laptop to a café. She said he spent more time chatting with his friends—"cronies" she called them—than doing serious work.

Clare looked over the piles of papers on Richard's desk. There were stacks of printouts of data on terrapins and scraps of hand-scrawled notes anchored by smooth beach rocks. At the back of the desk were two photographs in acrylic frames. She hadn't noticed them before. The large one was of a group of high school students who were winners of a California state science fair competition (the kids were holding up a sign announcing it), posing with their teacher. Clare looked over the faces of the kids, who were around her age. She wondered which was the one that her father knew.

The other photo was taken on the beach. A man was walking with a toddler in front of him, her arms were held up over her head and he held her two hands in his. It took Clare a moment to realize that the little girl in the photograph was herself. Although his face was angled down to look at the child, she could tell the man was Richard. He looked like the man in other photographs she had of him when he was younger, though this was a photograph she had never seen. It was a moment from her life that she did not remember, but a moment that had happened, for here was the evidence of it. In the photograph she was plunging forwards, a little white beach hat perched on the back of her head, the chin strap dangling around her neck. She had a gleeful expression, as if she was excited about taking those big steps. Clare wondered who was the photographer, the person she had been smiling at. Vera? Or her grandmother? Or someone else, entirely. Someone else, lost to the past.

Clare put the photograph back on the desk. There was a fine line of dust along the top curved edge of the acrylic. This wasn't a photograph that Richard had put out because he knew she was coming, but a photograph that lived on his desk.

She looked again at the photograph of the kids at the science fair. There were nine of them—five boys and four girls—all smiling. She studied their faces—especially those of the girls—trying to guess which was the one Richard was connected to. Was it the girl with the wire-frame glasses or the girl who was caught with her hand adjusting her collar? Richard had disappeared from Clare's life, but he had been part of the life of one of these kids, and none of them were his own daughter. She felt jealous of whoever it was—in fact she felt jealous of all of them. She set the photo back on the desk, but pushed it a little to the right, so it was partially blocked by the printer.

There were no photographs of Richard anywhere visible in Vera's house; there never had been. All the photographs were buried in albums or shoeboxes. And now there were no photographs of Peter visible, either. Soon, Clare guessed, there would be a photograph of

Vera and Tertio, on their wedding day—a tasteful, artistic photograph, of course.

***

When Richard came back, his face was radiant. He didn't look at all like the man who had been leaning over by the side of the car the night before, clutching his chest.

"I found a new nest this morning," he said. "I put a stick there to mark it but we'll go together now and set up the cage."

Clare ran upstairs to grab her sunglasses and then she and Richard hiked out to the beach. Richard was carrying the cage, and he'd given her a stake with a blue flag on the top. She felt like a kid in a parade.

Richard set down the cage at the base of the low dunes near the boathouse, then led Clare down towards the water. "Here are the tracks," he said. "This is how I found the nest." He pointed out the J-shaped prints set about eight inches apart, made by the turtle's feet, and the straight line in the center made by her dragging tail. "She came up from the water right here, made her way up the beach," said Richard. Clare followed the tracks just behind Richard. She would never have noticed them if she hadn't known what she was looking for.

In the grassy area on top of the low dunes the tracks seemed to end. "Here's a false nest," said Richard. "She dug her hole, didn't like it, and moved on." They followed the tracks farther along. Eventually Richard stopped. "Here's the spot," he said.

The slight disturbance in the sand could have been anything. It certainly wasn't easy to read the few clues, to imagine that this was a place where a turtle had dug a hole, laid her eggs, and buried them all neatly, covering the spot so there were few traces visible.

"Is there really something down there?" Clare asked.

Richard knelt in the sand and started scooping away the sand. "Take a look," he said.

In a depression, about half a foot underground, there was a clutch of small pale eggs. Richard lifted one carefully. "Hold out your hand," he said. He laid the egg gently in Clare's palm. She touched it cautiously with her finger. It wasn't like a bird's egg, but something that seemed more alive, with a shell that was soft and translucent.

"It's amazing a baby turtle's inside here."

"It will be."

Clare laid the egg down with the others, and she and Richard covered them up with the sand, just as the mother turtle had done. Richard set the cage over the spot and buried its rim, and Clare poked the stake into the sand. The blue flag fluttered.

"At the end of summer the hatchlings will peck their way out of those eggs," said Richard, "and make their way down to the marsh."

"How will they get out of the cage?"

"We check the nest sites every day and lift the cages off when the hatchlings emerge."

Clare ran her finger along the wire of the cage. She was glad it was there, keeping the eggs safe until they were ready.

Richard was looking out at the water. He turned to her now.

"About last night," he said. "I want to explain it to you. Do you know anything about panic attacks?"

"Sort of."

"They can be triggered by associations. When I

saw the mailbox and the kid on the bike, it brought back something that happened—it's not something I tell most people, but it's something I think you should know." He hesitated, and Clare could see that he was taking a moment to work out his wording in his head. When he continued, he spoke quickly, as if he were reciting, for the first time, something he'd learned by heart.

"A friend of mine commuted to work by bicycle. He had just gotten home and was standing over his bicycle getting his mail out of the mailbox. A car was speeding along the road and hit him. Killed him. End of story."

"I'm sorry," said Clare.

"Yup," said Richard. He stood up and brushed the sand from his hands.

12

In the afternoon Richard had work he wanted to do at his desk. Clare said she was fine going to the beach alone. She decided to wear her newest bathing suit, but she covered it with a T-shirt and draped a beach towel over her shoulders. She walked to the other end of the island to the cove where people swam. The small cluster of beach umbrellas—hot pink and turquoise and yellow stripes—looked festive, though a little jarring against the background of pale sand and beach grass. There were two boys digging in the sand, but no one was in the water, so Clare spent some time beachcombing, instead. She walked around the tip of the island, past the people, and then started back again. She noticed a girl her age ambling in her direction along the edge of the water, but didn't acknowledge that she'd seen her. But the girl was more gregarious. Once she spotted Clare she changed her course so she was headed right towards her. Clare stood where she was. As the girl approached, she gave a little wave. She was a few inches shorter than Clare and had an abundance of thick, bushy hair held up with an elastic, and a plump face that made her look, Clare guessed, probably a lot happier than she really was.

She introduced herself just the way Vera would do, holding out her hand and giving Clare's hand a squeeze.

"Hi, I'm Jaylin, J-A-Y-L-I-N," she said. "I always spell it because people never seem to get it right. Someone even once thought I said, 'Caitlin'."

"I'm Clare," said Clare. "No 'i'."

"That's a relief," said Jaylin, and she smiled. "Are you staying here on the island?"

"Yes," said Clare.

"Do you have a house here?"

"Well, my Dad does."

"My parents built a house," said Jaylin, "and dragged me here last summer. And there's no one around who isn't ancient or a little kid except for Mark—my brother—and his friends, and they don't count. How come I didn't see you last summer?"

"I wasn't here. I haven't been since I was little."

"Lucky you," said Jaylin. "I hope you're here for a while this time, because I'm stuck here for two more weeks."

"I'll be here," said Clare.

"Sweet," said Jaylin. "We can hang out together."

"Sure," said Clare.

"What are you collecting?" asked Jaylin, looking at Clare's hands.

Clare held out her open palm. "Whatever looks interesting," she said.

"Last summer I was obsessed with collecting scallop shells. I'm not anymore, but there's nothing much to do on this beach, so sometimes I still pick them up." Clare noticed Jaylin's gold bracelet. It seemed crazy that someone would wear something expensive like that on the beach.

"I don't know which shells are which," said Clare, "but I thought I could look them up. There's a shell book at the house."

"Where's your house?"

"Back there," said Clare, pointing vaguely towards the marsh.

"We're right up there," said Jaylin. The house she pointed to was a big one, perched on the top of the dune with decks hanging off in all directions. "Hey, why don't you come up with me and we can get something to drink, or some ice cream, OK?"

"OK," said Clare. She wondered if she should ask Richard or at least let him know, but there was no way to do that. If she was staying long at Jaylin's she could call him from the phone in Jaylin's house.

There was a long wooden staircase leading up to the house.

"The stairs are brand new this week," said Jaylin. "They almost didn't get it done in time. My mom was going to have a fit."

They paused at the landing halfway up and Clare looked out at the view of the bay. "The stairs we had last year got washed away in a storm," continued Jaylin. "Everything gets washed away here. The house is going to get washed away if we don't get a sea wall built. There's this crazy old guy on the island who's got this thing about sea walls. It's costing my dad a fortune in lawyers."

Crazy old guy. It took Clare a second to realize that it must be Richard whom Jaylin was talking about. Clare sat on the built-in bench on the landing.

"Hey, you're not that tired, are you?" asked Jaylin.

Clare shook her head. She thought about saying something about the turtles, but then Jaylin would want to know how she knew, and what would Jaylin think if she knew who Clare's father was? Still, he wasn't really crazy, and he wasn't that old, either.

"We're halfway up. Think ice cream!" said Jaylin. Clare wavered, her allegiances divided, but then Jaylin seized her hand and gave her a friendly tug and it tipped the balance. She followed Jaylin up the second half of the staircase. From the top she could see all the way from one side of the island to the other.

Everything in Jaylin's house was oversized: the rooms, the sofas, the windows, the view. It was the sort of house Vera liked, Clare thought, the new Vera, that is, the one who had chosen to live with Tertio instead of Peter. Peter had had what he called his "little extravagances"—like his ergonomic desk chair and his collection of fountain pens—but they'd lived in a modest house. Though Clare wondered now—and the thought seemed almost traitorous to Peter—if it was because Peter really had contempt for big, fancy houses, or if it was because he and Vera hadn't been able to afford anything better at the time.

Jaylin's house seemed dazzling inside. Everything was white, and the high ceilings were punctured with skylights so the rooms were filled with sunshine. Richard's small house in the shade seemed, in contrast, like a hobbit's hole.

Jaylin's room was all white, too, but there were spots of color: a pair of jeans thrown over the back of a chair, magazines half-stuck under the bed, an orange bathing suit top dangling from the closet doorknob. Jaylin seemed unconcerned about dripping ice cream on her white futon when she flopped down on it, but Clare stood by the window and finished her ice cream, careful not to get any on the carpeting, also white.

"Do you have twenty bucks you can lend me?" The voice came from a boy, a few years older than Jaylin, who had stuck his head in the doorway. His hair was bushy, like Jaylin's, and he had a rectangle of dark hair on his chin which looked like an attempt at a beard.

"Sorry, I'm totally broke," said Jaylin. "Why don't you ask Mom?"

"I don't know where she is."

"That's Mark, whom I have the misfortune to be related to," Jaylin said to Clare, and to him, she added, "Guess you'll have to hit up Dad, then."

"The dragon's in his lair," said Mark and he disappeared from the doorway.

Jaylin sucked the last bit of ice cream off her spoon and smiled at Clare. "My Dad's not really a dragon," she said. "He's just a temperamental writer who snaps at his poor offspring when he's having trouble coming up with ideas."

"My stepfather is a writer, too," said Clare.

"What does he write?"

"He's working on a novel. But he's published a lot of short stories." Clare pictured the two literary magazines Peter had been so proud of, and the online magazine. "A lot" wasn't actually exactly accurate, but it sounded much better than "a few."

"Dad writes crime thrillers," said Jaylin. "He writes the novel. And then the book becomes a best seller, so he writes the screenplay; then it gets made into a movie. Have you heard of *The Breaking Point*?"

Clare shook her head.

"*First and Ever After*?"

"I think so," said Clare, though she wasn't sure she had. Vera had as much contempt for "airport books" as she did for YA novels.

"This island is crawling with writers," said Jaylin.

Clare was about to explain that it was her real father who was here on the island, and her stepfather was somewhere else, but it immediately got too complicated. She'd have to explain that she didn't live with Peter anymore; she lived with her mother's third husband, Tertio, but that Peter was still her stepfather—because he was, wasn't he?

She wondered if she started off her relationship with Jaylin by not really telling her how things were, with a whole chunk of what was central to her life kept secret, would they ever have the possibility of a real friendship? If Jaylin thought her father was a writer, she wouldn't think he was that "crazy old guy." But that meant Jaylin couldn't ever come over to Richard's house, because then she would not only figure out the truth, but she'd discover that Clare hadn't been quite honest with her.

There was a man standing in the living room looking out at the view when Clare was leaving the house. He looked as old as Richard, but his greying hair was in a long ponytail. He was wearing loose-fitting clothes that might have been pajamas.

"Hi, Dad," said Jaylin. "This is Clare."

"Ahoy!" said Jaylin's dad, and he held up his wineglass in greeting.

"If Mark gets to take the boat to Provincetown I get to go, too, don't I?" Jaylin asked.

"That sounds reasonable to me," said her father.

"Will you tell him that, please?"

"When I have the opportunity."

"Can Clare come, too?"

"I don't see why not," said Jaylin's father.

Outside on the deck Jaylin turned to Clare. "That's great," she said. "It looks like we'll be going on Friday, as long as the weather's nice. You'll be able to come, won't you?"

Clare noted that Jaylin hadn't asked her if she wanted to come. Perhaps the answer was too obvious: of course she'd want to.

"I'll have to ask my dad first," she said. It seemed odd to be referring to him as her "dad," but surely it would seem odder to Jaylin if she called him "Richard."

Before Clare left, Jaylin wrote Clare's phone number down on a pad of paper shaped like a shell, and because Clare hadn't brought anything to write on, she wrote Jaylin's number on the back of her hand with a ballpoint pen.

"That's my house number," said Jaylin. "There's no cell reception here."

"I know."

"It's like the dark ages," said Jaylin. She stood at the top of the staircase and waved to Clare when Clare turned to look back up at the landing. But when Clare got to the bottom of the staircase and looked up again, Jaylin had left.

***

When Clare got back to the house Richard was still at his desk. He looked as if he hadn't moved from his chair the whole time she was away.

"We had a nice piece of good luck while you were gone," he said. "Someone renting out here spotted a turtle laying her eggs in the middle of a dirt road in front of their house and called the terrapin hotline—we'd given out notices to everyone on the island—and Steffi and her team were able to get out there and relocate the nest."

"That's great," said Clare.

"What happened to your hand?" asked Richard.

"Oh, that's just ink. I met a girl on the beach and we might do something together and that's her phone number."

"Good. You made a friend," said Richard.

"Made a friend" was what you'd say about a kid at the playground. And besides, Jaylin could hardly be counted as friend, certainly not yet. But Clare didn't say so to Richard.

"I guess I'll go change out of my bathing suit," she said. She went upstairs to her room and added Jaylin's number to the contacts on her cell phone.

Her phone might be useless for calls, but at least she could store numbers there. She scrolled through her contacts, looking at all the names. She had a lot of friends, but most of them were friends that she never talked with about anything that mattered a whole lot; most of them thought things were better in her life than they really were. It was only her friend Susannah who knew how much she missed Peter and how she felt when Vera decided to marry Tertio. It was only Susannah—Susannah, who was stuck in Colorado for the summer, practically the other side of the whole country—who knew how she'd felt about being shipped off to this island to spend three weeks with a man who was, it was true, her father, but who was really a stranger.

She went to the bathroom to wash the ink off her hand. She ran the cake of soap across her hand and rubbed the spot with her thumb. Even after two soapings and two rinses she couldn't get all the ink off. You couldn't read the number anymore, but you could tell that something had been written there.

Once Clare had come home from school with someone's phone number written on her arm and

Vera had been upset. She'd said it looked like the number the Nazis had tattooed on the Jews in the concentration camps, and it would be distressing to Ian, who was Jewish. She also said that the ink could cause a problem for Clare's skin. Vera never had just one reason for anything.

13

It rained the next day and there was rain promised for the day after. Jaylin called to tell Clare they were going into Boston and staying in a hotel for a few days and asked if she wanted to come. Clare might have considered asking Richard if she could go if she still felt as she did when she first got to Blackfish Island, but now she declined right away. The point of coming to Blackfish Island was to spend time with Richard, not to be escaping to somewhere else.

"How come you're going to Boston?" she asked.

"My mom is hungry for some urban time and my dad needs some undisturbed time," Jaylin explained.

"And Mark has some friend who's flying in to Logan so we'll meet up with him and then he'll come back and spend a week here."

"That's nice," said Clare.

"Nice!" cried Jaylin. "My brother gets to have a friend from home come and visit, but not me. 'Next summer,' is what my mom said. She'd better believe I'll hold her to that next year."

"Where's home?" asked Clare, changing the subject.

"Philadelphia," said Jaylin. "An unfortunate distance from the Cape—just close enough so my insane parents think it driving distance. So I have to spend a hundred hideous hours in the car. Where are you from?"

"New York," said Clare. "Not exactly New York, just the suburbs outside of it."

"Lucky you. No wonder you don't want to go into Boston," said Jaylin. "I'll see you when I'm back. And don't forget about the trip to P-Town."

Clare hadn't mentioned the trip to Richard because she didn't know how serious Jaylin's invitation was, but now she thought she better ask him if she could go. He was working at his desk and when she came into his room he pushed his reading glasses halfway down his nose and looked at her over the top of them. Vera would have had a hundred questions and probably would have wanted to speak to Jaylin's mother before she gave her consent. But Richard just nodded and said, "If that's what you'd like to do."

It was a relief not to have to explain anything. Still it might have been nice if he'd asked Clare at least one question, just to show he was interested in what she was doing.

***

The rain weighed down the branches of the oak trees close by the house, and the lichens on the trunks of the pitch pine had a silvery hue against the rain-dark trunks. Mist muted the view of the marsh. It felt as if they were in a forest, not near a beach by the sea. But at low tide the island asserted itself. The woodsy smell of pine needles and humus was eclipsed by the smell of the marsh. And even if you couldn't see the bay, you knew it was close by.

Clare walked the beach with Richard twice a day, but they didn't spot any more turtle tracks. In the evening Richard dug out some old board games which he said had been in the house for as long as he could remember.

"When we were out here in the summer, we had no TV, no video games—my mother liked it that way," he said. He smiled. "I got used to it."

The Parcheesi set had black cardboard cylindrical shakers that were missing their bottoms, so you had to cup your hand over it when it was your turn to roll the dice. Because there were only two players, they each played two colors. Clare's red and yellow came in second and third. Richard's blue was first.

The Chinese checkers board was beautifully carved wood, but Richard wasn't able to find the box of marbles that went with it. The only marbles he did find was an odd assortment in an oatmeal container. Richard spilled them out on a tray.

"My old collection," he said, and he nudged them affectionately with his forefinger. They were different sizes and colors, some clear as glass, some opaque as stone. Clare held an apricot-sized green one up to the light. When you looked through it, it was like being under the sea.

Because there weren't enough matching marbles to make a set, Richard proposed using peas. "Peas against marbles," he said, and he brought out a paper bag of peas from the refrigerator and a bowl to shell them in. They ate the ones too small for playing with. The peas lined up in the dimples of wood made Clare giggle, but Richard played very seriously, concentrating on the board as if he were in a professional chess tournament, not a man studying a battlefield army of mismatched marbles and unevenly sized green peas. Richard proved to be an amazing jumper. His peas followed ingenious zigzag routes to reach their destination.

"I don't know how you can see those moves," said Clare. Richard ran through his eight-jump move in slow motion for her.

"The trick is you have to be willing to go backwards to find a path forwards. Most players are so fixed on advancing their pieces that they don't explore those longer, backwards routes."

"You mean me?"

Richard smiled. "You. And everyone else. I was a crack Chinese checkers player when I was a kid. It was a winning strategy I learned from my father. It's a strategy of the old, the patient. Kids never get it."

"You didn't have any brothers or sisters, right?"

"No," said Richard. "I was an only child, just like you."

"How come?"

"What do you mean how come?"

"I'm an only child because, well, because Mom and you weren't married that long. And then I guess Peter wasn't ready to have kids—or . . . I don't know. " Clare wasn't really sure. Maybe it was because Vera didn't want to have kids with Peter.

"My mother had two miscarriages before she had me. And when she finally got her perfect baby—she called me that, but of course I wasn't really *perfect*," Richard smiled broadly at this—"she decided that was enough." Richard paused for a moment. "Do you like being an only child?" he asked.

"It's OK," said Clare. "How about you?"

"When I was kid, yes, it seemed OK. As an adult, when my life got hard, I would have liked to have had a sibling to share that with. And when my parents died—within half a year of each other—I had no one to grieve with me."

There was quiet all around them. Clare wanted to know what he meant by his life getting hard. It seemed like it was an opening to something, to some of the questions she wanted to ask, but she wasn't sure how to begin. She ran her finger along the row of marbles on the board in front of her. Then she looked up at him.

"What was hard?" she asked.

Richard looked as if he had expected this question, perhaps he had even drawn it out from her, yet he also seemed as if he didn't know how he was going to answer.

"I made some changes in my life—or rather, my life took me in directions I hadn't anticipated."

Clare kept her eyes on the Chinese checkers. She felt suddenly afraid now, as if she was about to hear something she might not want to hear, and she was sorry she had begun this. And yet, maybe she wasn't.

"Was that when you moved to the West Coast?" she asked.

"Actually, it was after that. I relocated to California when you were three," said Richard. "I was working in computers then and got involved with an Internet start-up company out there. Vera and I were having a trial separation. I thought I'd be out there for only a while, see how things went."

Clare looked up at Richard now.

"The company took off. Vera decided she wanted to marry Peter. So I had to decide if I was going to return to the East Coast or make my life out there."

Clare waited.

"It seemed simpler to stay out there," said Richard.

Clare felt as if she had been slapped. "What about me?" she asked.

Richard stood up. At first she thought he was going to walk off, leave her question behind. But instead he stretched and rubbed his hands through his hair. Then he sat down again.

"You've gotten to the core problem, haven't you? What to do about you. I decided—and perhaps I was wrong about this—that it was better for you if I stayed out of your life completely. Vera and Peter seemed to be a stable parental unit, and I wanted you to have that. Have them."

So he had given her Peter. She would never have thought about it that way, would never have imagined that her relationship with Peter was at all dependent on

Richard's generosity. But even so, he had abandoned her. He'd supported her financially, but he'd gone off and left her behind.

"I always thought that you just didn't want to see me," said Clare.

Richard shook his head slowly. "No," he said. "That wasn't it."

"You never visited once, my entire childhood—years and years."

"I didn't want you to grow up with divided loyalties. I didn't want you to feel confused."

"I wouldn't have been confused. My friend Susannah has a stepfather but she sees her real father a lot, too, and he lives in Colorado. And that's a lot better than not seeing him at all." She couldn't keep the anger out of her voice.

"I'm sorry, Clare," said Richard quietly. "There were reasons that I thought it was better—there were certain difficulties. I cared for you a great deal, and I did what I thought was best—please believe me—given the situation at the time."

"And now? What's different now?"

"You're older; things have changed. I've been trying

to arrange for you to visit since I moved back East two years ago. I wanted you to know that I did want to see you, all those years. I wanted you to understand that." He stopped and seemed to gather himself. "And there's something else, too."

Clare's fear came back. There was something else. But maybe Richard didn't really want to talk about it. And maybe she didn't have to know it, not if she didn't want to.

Richard lifted the peas from the board and dropped them back in the bowl. Clare picked up the marbles and dropped them, one at a time, back in the box, where they clicked against the marbles that hadn't been used. Glass against glass.

If you didn't want to know things, you didn't have to know them. Things didn't become facts until someone actually spoke them. Until then, you could just go on acting just the way you had been acting and even if you suspected there was something that would change everything, you didn't have to acknowledge it; you didn't have to let it in.

14

Diamondback terrapins, Clare learned from Richard, came up into estuaries to feed at high tide, and returned to the bay at low tide. If you wanted to catch them you needed to do that from kayaks at high tide, or net them as they swam out across a narrow channel as the tide went out. Every terrapin caught was marked, measured, recorded, then released.

"What's the point of that?" asked Clare.

"We don't know much about these creatures," said Richard. "We're collecting data so we can learn about them—we need to learn about them so we can figure out the best ways to protect them."

Richard gave Clare a net with a long aluminum handle and they set out in the kayaks for a cove Richard called "the terrapin singles bar," where turtles met potential mates. It didn't take Clare long to get used to handling a kayak again, and she felt like an authentic naturalist, not just someone paddling around for fun, with the net propped in the kayak next to her. She kept up with Richard paddling to the cove. He checked over his shoulder to make sure she was close behind, but he didn't seem to slow his pace for her benefit. In the field he became a man of purpose, his eye on the goal ahead. Clare was relieved when they reached the cove and came on shore at a small beach, where Richard unloaded his equipment.

"We'll circle around the perimeter once and see what's happening," said Richard. "Let me know if you see a turtle. Look underwater and also watch for its head. They have to come up to breathe."

"What if it's a snapping turtle?" asked Clare.

"They're in freshwater; this is salt," said Richard. "The only turtles here would be our babies."

When they were back out in their kayaks Richard demonstrated how to use the net. "The trick is to swoop it under the terrapin, but keep your center of gravity so you don't tip your kayak."

"What do I do with the paddle?"

"Tuck it next to you. And if you go over, it's OK. You've done it before and it's no problem."

Except for getting back into the kayak again. But she didn't say anything.

Richard had her do some practice sweeping with her net, then they started off. Clare paddled behind him, scanning the water on both sides of her kayak. In places the angle was wrong and the sun glared on the surface, giving a reflection rather than a window through. They were up in a small inlet when Richard cried out, "Got one coming towards us on the right." Clare studied the water, but didn't see anything.

He popped up in his seat, did a quick maneuver with his kayak, swooshing his net and paddling so fast that Clare couldn't make out what was happening.

"Lost her," he said after a bit, and he sat back in his seat. They paddled farther along, but didn't spot that terrapin again, or any others. After a while Richard suggested Clare continue hunting where they were, and he was going to check things out across the cove.

"This way we can cover twice the territory," he said. "If you see anything, give a shout."

"But I shouldn't try to catch one, should I?" asked Clare. She was rather hoping he'd say no.

"If you feel up to it, and have an easy shot, give it a try," he said.

"And what do I do with it if I catch it?"

"Drop it in the bottom of the kayak and I'll be right over."

Too soon he was paddling off and Clare was on her own. She paddled slowly parallel to the shore. She saw something that looked like a turtle head and paddled fast towards it, but it proved to be only a stick. And something she spotted moving underwater turned out to be a horseshoe crab. Still, it was pleasant bobbing in the kayak and when she was paddling where it was shallow, the long grasses made a lovely rustling sound as they brushed the bottom of the boat. She was tired now. When she came to a quiet inlet she decided to have a rest. She put her paddle beside her and took a long drink from her water bottle. She pulled her legs out up on top of the kayak. Her life jacket was hot and she unzipped it halfway, but she thought Richard might be a stickler about such things so she zipped it back up again.

Richard was a small figure moving along the far shore of the cove. How different he seemed today from the night before. It was as if they hadn't talked about anything. Maybe it was only when the house was muffled by darkness and rain that they were able to talk with each other. In the open sunshine Richard was a man who seemed to have no interest in talking, a man who was involved with terrapins, but nothing more. It was a relief, too, in a way, Clare thought. Out here, in her kayak on the water, she could almost forget that there was something that she had chosen not to know. It was still there, but maybe she could outwait it, and it would just disappear.

The water here was calm and the surface was unrippled. It was like looking through the glass of an aquarium. A spider crab picked its way along the bottom. A school of silvery fish, small as dimes, darted around the grasses. Suddenly Clare spotted a turtle— it was unquestionably a turtle. It was swimming in a leisurely way, right alongside her kayak, totally unaware of her. It was a big turtle, twice as big as any of the painted turtles on Tertio's pond, and it looked just like the terrapin whose picture Richard had showed her on his computer. She forgot entirely that she was supposed to try to catch it; she forgot, even, to call out and let Richard know that it was there. She was entirely caught up in watching it. What fascinated her was how graceful it was, how it moved so effortlessly through the water, just by stroking with its feet. It was a remarkable design, this turtle, a perfectly balanced buoyancy. Although it looked like a creature that would be rock-heavy, it did not sink to the bottom, nor was it so light it rose, as if inflated, to the surface. It navigated through the water with the confidence of a fish, holding its breath so long that it was easy to forget that it was a creature who, just like her, needed to breathe the air. It swam underneath her kayak, but when she looked for it over the other side, it had disappeared so completely that it was easy to believe she had just imagined it.

When she looked up to call Richard she saw that he was already paddling towards her across the cove.

"I saw one," she told him. "It was right here—but I was watching it and forgot to try to catch it. I'm sorry."

Richard smiled. "That happens," he said. "But come with me back to the beach now; I've got two that need to be measured."

"You've got two?" Clare exclaimed. "Where are they?"

"Right here," said Richard, and he pointed down inside his kayak.

Suddenly Clare spotted the head of a turtle pop up just in front of them. "There's one," she cried, and pointed. The head popped down back under the water, but Richard had seen it, too. He was after it in a flash.

"Get your net ready!" he called. "She's heading towards you."

It happened so quickly that Clare didn't know how she actually did it. Some instinct had taken over and in a second she'd spotted the turtle, reached out with her net, and the next thing she knew she was struggling to hold on to the weight at the end of her net and keep her kayak from tipping over. Richard's kayak was beside hers in an instant.

"Great job!" he said.

The turtle was a clawing, thrashing creature, big as a dinner plate and heavy as a rock. It scratched Clare's arm and she almost dropped it, net and all. Richard got it out of the net and held it for her to see. Clare stared at it and it stared right back at her. It had a wild, prehistoric look, like a dinosaur or a dragon.

"Isn't she a beauty?" Richard asked.

They brought the terrapin back to shore and Richard got out his equipment for measuring and marking them.

"Yours is a female," he told Clare. "They're always bigger than the males. And she's one who's never been captured before. We'll do her first." Richard showed Clare how to hold the turtle so it couldn't claw her, but it was difficult to hold on to that heavy weight and keep her hands free of the sharp claws.

"Steady, Sweetheart," he said to the turtle.

"What happened to her shell here?" asked Clare.

Richard rubbed the damaged spot with his thumb. "Got hit by something," he said. "Probably a boat propeller, but it's healed up fine. It isn't slowing her down."

The turtle didn't like to be weighed. She didn't like to be measured with calipers. And she did not like having the edge of her shell notched with a file.

It seemed like a cruel procedure to Clare, but Richard assured her it didn't actually hurt the turtle. Every turtle had a different series of notches that stood for numbers, this was #1430 and it would be entered in the database.

"This little lady's gravid," said Richard.

"What's that?" asked Clare.

"Full of eggs. She's going to be coming up on the shore any day now to lay them. Here, you can feel them inside her."

Richard held the turtle and showed Clare where to slip her fingers in the back, between the shells. It seemed like too intimate a thing, an invasion of the turtle's privacy, but Clare didn't want to say so. And it was miraculous, after all, to reach in among the folds of turtle skin and feel something like marbles, which were the eggs the turtle would be laying, future baby turtles.

"Could we give her a name?" asked Clare. "I know she has a number, but wouldn't it be nice for her to have a name, too?"

"Certainly. What do you want to name her?" asked Richard.

Clare looked at the turtle. The turtle's eyes were bright and intelligent looking. She looked a bit like a photograph of Eleanor Roosevelt in Clare's social studies textbook.

"How about Eleanor?" she asked.

"That's fine by me," said Richard.

When they were done recording all the information about the turtle, Richard handed her over to Clare to take back down to the water to release.

"So, she's going to have to swim all the way out into the bay, and around Blackfish Island, watching out for boats, lobster traps, fishing nets, and all sorts of dangers, then climb across the beach and up to the dunes and find a place to lay her eggs?"

"That's the way it is," said Richard.

"Couldn't we just find a nice spot for her and take her there?"

Richard shook his head.

Clare held the turtle out at a safe distance and walked down the beach looking for the best place to put her down. She waded out into the water and picked a spot where there was nice eel grass to slither away into.

"OK, Eleanor," she said. "You're on your own."

She set the turtle down in the water and it scrambled out of her grasp before she had quite let go. Without looking back once the turtle took off, swimming just as fast and gracefully as the turtle Clare had spotted on the other side of the cove. She was gone in an instant.

"Good luck, Sweetheart!" cried Clare.

15

Clare helped Richard with the other two terrapins, and then she released them both into the bay. One was a male and the other was a female. The male was missing a back leg.

"Could have been bitten off by something or gotten caught in netting or rope and then he gnawed it off himself."

"That's horrible," said Clare.

Richard shrugged. "It happens. If turtles get tangled on something underwater they can drown. If they're desperate to get up to air they'll do anything. And this guy looks as if he's survived OK."

The female had been captured and marked before, #721. Later, back at the house, they went to Richard's study. Richard pulled up a chair so Clare could sit next to him at the desk and they could look at the screen together. They entered all the information about Eleanor and the male terrapin. They checked out #721 and found she had been tagged six years before and captured again a year ago after laying eggs on Blackfish Island.

"What happened to the nest?"

Richard flipped to a new screen on his computer and scrolled down. "We marked it and put a cage protector on it, but it seems the eggs didn't survive."

"Why not?"

"In this case, probably beach grass," he said. "The roots seek out moisture and nutrients and basically suck the eggs dry."

"You're kidding!" cried Clare.

"No," said Richard. "The grass roots are as dangerous as any predator. That's why we need those bare sandy places, those eroded dunes."

"What about Eleanor?" asked Clare. "She's going to be laying her eggs soon. What about her nest?"

"We do whatever we can for every nest we can find," said Richard. "That's the best we can do." He started shutting off his computer.

Clare sat there for a moment watching the screen go dark. Then her eyes moved to the photograph in the frame behind it.

"That's us, isn't it?" she asked, pointing.

Richard lifted the photo and set it closer to them on the desk. He nodded. "That was taken when you were here," he said. "It was always a battle to get Vera to come. She called it 'roughing it'—though we had hot water and indoor plumbing. Her idea of an island was Manhattan."

"Who took the picture?"

"My mother—your grandmother. She was always so happy to have us visit."

"I don't remember her at all," said Clare.

"I'm sorry about that," said Richard. "She would have loved to have known you the way you are now, all grown up."

"I don't really think of myself as all grown up," said Clare.

Richard laughed. "You know something, I don't

think of myself as all grown up, either. Especially now living in this house, where I'd spent so much time as a kid."

"Do you have other old photos?" asked Clare. "Photos from back then?"

"I'm sure there are some old albums around," said Richard. "I've never had occasion to dig them out, but I suppose it's the right time for that, while you're visiting, isn't it?"

Clare's eye moved to the other photograph on the desk. She felt the wave of jealousy come over her as it had when she'd first seen it. She wanted to tip the frame so the photo would be facedown on the desk, so whatever kid it was who had been part of her father's life when she had been exiled from it would be staring into the dark wood. But her curiosity was too strong. She reached for the photo and set it closer to them.

"Which is the kid you know in this picture?" she asked.

Richard's hand moved towards the photo frame and his fingers settled lightly along the edge. He looked at the photo for a long time. Then he looked at Clare. "I don't know any of the kids in the photo," he said. "The person I know in the photo was the teacher. His name was Charlie McNeil."

Clare looked at the man in the photo. He had dark hair that was falling across his forehead, a mustache, and a boyish, friendly look.

"He's not alive anymore?"

"No," said Richard softly.

"How come you have this photo?"

"It's the way I like to remember him. He loved teaching. He inspired his students to do great stuff. He really got them to care about achieving things, even students whom everyone else had given up on." Richard's voice filled with—what was it?—pride? Yes, pride, as if Charlie wasn't simply just a friend.

Then Clare knew. The idea hadn't occurred to her before. But now, looking back, she saw that there had been small hints, which she had observed but not actually noted. She didn't know how she knew, but she did. She'd been afraid to let herself think it, afraid to say it in her mind, but strangely, now that she knew, at least she wasn't afraid of it anymore.

She looked at Richard. They didn't say anything, but as they watched each other's faces it was all made clear. Clare saw that Richard could tell that she now had figured out what he had been wanting her eventually to know.

They sat there in such quiet that all Clare could hear was the plastic clock on Richard's desk. It made a thunking sound each time the second hand jumped from one dot to the next, like the beating of a heart.

16

At night, in her room upstairs, Clare turned off the lights and opened the window wide. The smell of the marsh was strong and constant, familiar to her now as the smell of her own body. She pressed her face against the screen and it bulged under the pressure, then flattened again as she leaned back a little. She bounced her forehead against the screen, stretching it in its metal frame. Each time, it resumed its flatness.

Somewhere, deep in the marsh, there was a melancholy three-note cry—some bird of night—repeated again, and once again. But no other bird answered it. Clare pulled back from the window.

She stretched out on her bed and closed her eyes and concentrated on the comforting smell of the marsh.

Once you knew something, you couldn't un-know it. It was there, always, and there wasn't any way you could tuck it away again, make it something that didn't exist.

It wasn't that Richard was different; it's just that something about Richard was different. Well, not that it *was* different, really, because it had been there, hadn't it, even if she hadn't realized it.

Yet how could it always have been there? Richard had been married to Vera. And Richard was her father, wasn't he? How could he have been married to Vera; how could he have had a child? It creeped her out, the whole thing. It didn't make sense.

But part of it did make sense. The part of it that had to do with what puzzled her before. What that woman Steffi had called Richard: "a man of many secrets."

The idea of what Richard was had formed in her mind, but she hadn't allowed herself to use a word to describe it. Now she confronted the words. It was one thing to consider the terminology in general—

something else entirely to find a term for her own father. "Homosexual" sounded like something out of a pamphlet on sexuality from her school health class. "Gay" sounded like something frivolous, unserious, not like Richard at all. But what would you call it if you didn't call it that?

Clare tried to think about men she knew who were gay. There were actors of course, and the blond singer who came out and everyone at school was talking about it. But in her own life? The only people she could think of were a few kids who were in the Gay-Straight Alliance, and she didn't know them very well, and Monsieur Langlois, her seventh grade French teacher, and she hadn't even figured it out on her own. She'd always thought he was really cute, and she'd been envious of Ms. Miransky, who taught social studies, because they were always hanging out and laughing and once she'd seen them together in a restaurant in the city. When she'd asked Susannah if she thought they were living together Susannah had said, "Come on, Clare, Monsieur Langlois is gay."

"How do you know?" she'd asked.

"Everyone knows," Susannah had said.

"That's not a reason," she had insisted. "Maybe it's just that he's French. French men aren't like Americans."

"Oh, Clare," Susannah had said. "Don't be so naïve."

Vera was certainly outspoken in favor of gay rights, but that didn't tell Clare how Vera really felt about people who were gay. Peter had a friend who was a lesbian, a poet in his writing group, whom Vera didn't like very much, and once when they were arguing about something about her Peter had accused Vera of being homophobic. Vera had been furious. "Marcia's sexual orientation has absolutely nothing to do with it," she'd shouted. "That woman is a dreadful poet with an enormous ego. And whenever your writing group meets at the house she never brings even a bag of chips, but she eats everything in sight."

Clare wondered if Vera had any idea that Richard was gay. And what would her response be if she found out now? Not that Clare had any intention of telling her.

There was so much Clare didn't know about all

of this, but there wasn't anyone she could ask. There wasn't anyone she could talk to about any of this. Not Susannah. Not even Aunt Eva. She was stuck with this, and it was hers alone. Hers and Richard's.

17

In the morning when Clare came downstairs Richard had glass of orange juice and a cereal bowl and spoon laid out at her place on the table. He looked exactly the same, the way he'd looked every morning since she had arrived—the same blue shirt, the same shorts, the same tanned arms. There was nothing different about him at all, except for this fact that she now knew about. It seemed that it should have changed everything, but strangely, nothing seemed to have changed. They ate breakfast and talked about terrapins, and by the time she was putting the milk back into the refrigerator she had almost forgotten what had happened the night before. Almost forgotten what irrevocable knowledge was now hers.

Jaylin called not long after breakfast to say that they were back and to ask Clare to come over.

"Mark's friend Kip is here and I'm entirely out-numbered," she wailed.

Clare guessed that Jaylin wanted to see her only because she had no one else, and not because Jaylin liked her in particular. But she did want to get away from the house—from Richard, from everything. And if Jaylin was inviting her because there was nobody else to hang around with, that was true about her, too: *she* had no one else to hang out with. If Susannah or any of her own friends from home were here she wouldn't even have met Jaylin in the first place. So as long as the relationship was even that way, it didn't matter, did it?

Richard didn't mind her going off for the day. And he didn't ask any questions about where, exactly, she was going. "I'll make dinner around six," he said. "You like grilled fish, don't you?

"Sure," said Clare.

When she went over to Jaylin's, Mark and Kip were in the garage where a Ping-Pong table took over one of the three places for cars.

"They won't play with me, but they'll play doubles with us," said Jaylin.

"I'm not very good at Ping-Pong," said Clare.

"That's all right," said Jaylin.

Mark was wearing a bandana tied pirate-style around his forehead to hold his hair back. He was sweating as if he were in a tennis match.

"I'm going finish Kip off," said Mark as he got ready to serve, "and then we'll take on the two of you."

"Like hell, you'll finish me off," said Kip, but he didn't turn around to look at them. He was not much taller than Clare, a head shorter than Mark, but not as skinny.

Clare and Jaylin watched the end of the game. The ball moved faster than Clare had ever seen before. It skimmed the net. Clare's stomach tightened.

It was Kip who beat Mark. Mark threw his paddle on the table and shouted, "Shit! I can't believe I blew it. One more game!"

"No way!" yelled Jaylin. "I've been waiting to play for hours and if you're not going to do doubles then it's my turn with the Ping-Pong table."

"Time to take on your sister," said Kip. Mark picked up his paddle and Kip moved around to his side of the table. Kip's hair was straight and sandy colored, and his eyes were so dark you couldn't see the outline of the pupils.

"This is my friend Clare," said Jaylin. "She's from New York."

"Not exactly," said Clare.

"Hey," said Kip. Clare's hand moved to the neckline of her T-shirt. She hadn't thought about what she was wearing when she left the house—it hadn't occurred to her that Mark's friend might be someone cute—and now she wished she'd worn something more flattering.

Jaylin got to serve first, and when Mark slammed the ball back it whizzed past Clare so quickly she didn't even have time to lift her paddle. On the next return it was only luck that she got her paddle in the right position. The ball went over the net but it was back before Clare could take a breath, touching a corner of the table that seemed a mile from where she was standing. Jaylin leaned far into Clare's side of the table to reach balls that Clare was obviously unable to hit. When it was Clare's turn to serve, her ball took a slow high arc that was immediately pounded down by Kip.

"You know," said Jaylin, "maybe we should do something else."

"I'm sorry," said Clare. "I told you I wasn't very good."

"That's OK; it's too hot for Ping-Pong, anyway. Let's go for a swim." Jaylin tossed the ball to her brother. "See you around, guys," she said.

"See you," said Kip, and Clare thought he actually smiled at her.

Clare had her bathing suit on under her clothes. She put her shorts and T-shirt in the beach bag she'd brought and left the bag on a chair on Jaylin's deck. They brought their towels with them and walked down Jaylin's long staircase and around to the swimming beach.

"I'm hot," said Jaylin. "Let's swim first and lie on the beach after." She didn't wait to hear Clare's response before she headed out to the water.

The water was clear and had a turquoise tint that was like the water in Bermuda where Clare had accompanied Vera and Tertio on what Vera called her "premarital honeymoon". The comparison was deceptive because the ocean in Bermuda had been so warm Clare had floated endlessly on her back, ignoring Vera and Tertio holding hands in lounge chairs on the beach, whereas here she waded out on tiptoe, feeling the cold move up her body in excruciating increments as she went in deeper. Once she was wet, though, it felt refreshing, and after she and Jaylin had swum for a while and done handstands, they floated companionably near each other on their backs.

"You really suck at Ping-Pong, don't you," said Jaylin after they'd come out of the water and stretched out on their towels.

"I *told* you," said Clare.

"Those guys are such jerks, anyway. Never mind them."

"I didn't mind them," said Clare.

"Well, you would, if you got stuck with Mark as a brother."

"What about Kip?" said Clare. She tried to pronounce his name as neutrally as possible.

"He's an idiot, too," said Jaylin. "All of my brother's friends are idiots. Do you have any brothers?"

"No," said Clare. "I'm an only child."

"Consider yourself blessed," said Jaylin. She raised herself on one elbow and looked at Clare.

"What?" Clare asked.

"I was trying to decide whether I should tell you something or not," said Jaylin.

Clare shrugged. She had the sense that Jaylin would have liked it if she had said, "please do" but she wasn't sure she wanted to have Jaylin confide in her. Jaylin's disappointment was brief. She sat up now and leaned towards Clare conspiratorially.

"I'm not supposed to tell anybody, but I'm going to tell you," said Jaylin. "I actually have another brother; his name is Daniel. He's two years younger than me, but he doesn't live with us. Something happened when he was born, and he was tragically impaired. So he lives in a special home for children like him."

"I'm sorry," said Clare.

"Oh, there's nothing to be sorry about," said Jaylin. "It's this really nice place with all these really nice people who take care of him." She smiled.

"Then how come you're not supposed to tell people?"

Jaylin shrugged. "It's my mom. She tried having Daniel live at home, but it turns out the person who was living with us to take care of him was really just interested in having my dad get her connections in the film industry, and so it didn't work. Besides, this is a lot better for Daniel."

There was a piece of logic missing here—the not-telling anyone part—but Clare decided not to pursue it. She doubted that she was the only person Jaylin had told this to—surely Jaylin had a number of friends at home who had each been singled out as confidante. She was afraid that Jaylin was going to expect some kind of compensatory confession from her, and there was nothing she wanted to tell Jaylin. Especially now. She was relieved when Jaylin leapt up after swatting at a greenhead fly.

"That's it!" she cried. "Time to abandon beach!"

Back at the house they made ice cream sodas. The house was tranquil. Jaylin checked the cars in the driveway and decided that Mark and Kip had probably gone off somewhere. Jaylin wanted to watch a video, but Clare said she thought she should be going back home.

"Don't forget Friday," said Jaylin. "We'll be leaving in the morning and we'll buy lunch in P-Town."

"OK," said Clare. Friday was a few days away and Clare noted that Jaylin didn't say anything about getting together before then. That was fine with her, too. She collected her things and walked down the flight of stairs to the beach. Once out of sight of Jaylin's deck, she walked more slowly. She wasn't in any particular hurry to get back to the house. Clare watched a group of sea ducks diving in the bay. They had tufts of feathers sticking out from the backs of their heads, as if they had been caught in the wind. Clare tried to count how long they stayed underwater. It was hard to tell though, because they didn't pop up in the same spot, but it was so long that each time she was afraid they might not make it.

When she came around the side of the island she noticed a figure in the distance, walking towards her. When they got closer she saw that it was Richard. If she didn't know him, would she think he was some crazy old guy? He did have grey hair, but he didn't walk like an old man; in fact, he had spotted her and was jogging towards her now, not the way men did when they were exerting themselves working out, but with an easy gait, the way a coyote might run.

And if she didn't know him, would there be anything about him that would make her think he was gay? There wasn't anything she noticed, but maybe she just wasn't very good at picking up on things like this; maybe there was something about Richard that other people could see.

"Your mother called," he said.

"Is everything OK?" Clare was suddenly frightened.

"Everything's OK at her end," said Richard, "but not so good at my end. I gather I have been negligent in my parental duties. I revealed not only my ignorance of where you were, but also the full name of the girl whom you were with. Your mother wants you to call her back as soon as you're at the house."

"I'm sorry," said Clare.

"No reason you should be sorry," said Richard. "Mea culpa, entirely. I didn't think to ask where, precisely, you would be. And I didn't find out this friend of yours last name. I just don't know much about taking care of teenagers, I guess. "

"That's OK."

They walked around the side of the island and cut up the path through the dunes back towards the house.

"I haven't talked to Vera for years—we've dealt with each other though letters and e-mail—and it was surprising to have her call out of the blue and to have her berate me. But I suppose I deserved it."

When they were back at the house Clare turned to Richard.

"Does Vera know?" she asked.

"Know what?"

"About you."

Richard thought for a moment. "The answer, Clare, is no; I don't believe she does."

"Is that why you stayed out there, in California? So no one would know?"

"No. I stayed because I had a good job out there. And later I stayed because of Charlie."

"But you didn't want people to know, right?"

"My friends out there all knew, of course, but there was no reason to tell Vera. She might have guessed if she'd put her mind to it. But Clare, the truth is that Vera had lots of other things that she put her mind to. As long as I sent her checks and didn't interfere with any of her decisions about you, things were the way she wanted them to be."

Richard went to the kitchen counter and gave Clare Vera's phone number.

"What should I say to her?"

Richard shrugged. "Whatever you want."

Vera's voice was high and excited. "I hope this hasn't all been a dreadful mistake," she said.

"I'm fine, Mom," said Clare. "There's nothing to be worried about. I'm having a good time."

It took some work to reassure Vera so she didn't call Eva to come to rescue Clare from Richard.

"I don't want to undermine your father's authority," said Vera, "but I'm concerned that he doesn't seem to be exercising any authority."

"I was just at a friend's house, right nearby," said Clare, stressing the word friend slightly more than was truthful. "It wasn't like I was doing anything danger-ous. We were playing Ping-Pong." Surely there was no reason to mention swimming.

Vera wanted to know all about Jaylin, and was audibly relieved, as Clare guessed she might be, when she learned that Jaylin's father was the author of best-selling novels that had been made into movies. Just saying he was a writer wouldn't do since Vera had been impatient with what she called Peter's "dilettantism." Clare seized this moment of softening to ask about France, and Vera, fears assuaged, was happy to describe for Clare all the pleasures and tribulations—for with Vera there were always tribulations—of the villa they had rented.

Through the window Clare watched Richard walking by, carrying a bowl of kitchen scraps out to the compost pile. She felt oddly protective of him. In a final gesture to appease Vera she asked after Tertio, careful to call him Ian.

18

Richard had been out on the deck, sitting in one of the faded canvas chairs. Clare thought for a moment that maybe he had been simply lounging there, watching the view, but noticed he had a book he laid by his side. It was, as she might have guessed, a serious book, on mollusks.

He looked up at her. "So," he asked, "what's the verdict?"

Clare opened the other chair and set it up beside him. "It's OK," she said. "I don't think we have anything to worry about. I've persuaded her that I'm not in grave danger, so she's not flying home to rescue me, and she's not calling Eva, either."

"Thank you, Clare," said Richard. "I guess that although she doesn't trust me, she trusts you. I don't think that I will live up to Vera's exacting parental standards, but I will try to be more vigilant."

"I like the way you've been," said Clare. "Mom's not exactly easy to live with, you know."

"Oh, I know," said Richard.

Clare slipped her feet out of her flip-flops and stretched her legs out in front of her.

"Aunt Eva says you and Mom weren't a match made in heaven," said Clare.

Richard laughed. "I guess not," he said.

"But what I don't understand," said Clare, "is how come you were married at all. I mean, I just don't get it." Clare trailed off.

"Is this something you'd like to talk about?" asked Richard.

"I guess so," said Clare.

"How about you just ask me any questions you want, and I'll do my best to answer them?"

"Then you should be able to ask any question about me, too," said Clare. "You haven't really asked me anything since I've been here."

"Haven't I?" Richard seemed surprised.

Clare shook her head. "Not at all. I'd expected you'd ask me lots of questions."

"What kind of questions?"

"Like 'what do you want to do when you grow up' kind of questions."

"Are you disappointed?"

"Not really," said Clare. "Older people are always asking me those kind of questions, and I never know what to answer."

Richard leaned forwards and reached around his chair to set the backrest a notch lower so he was level with Clare. They were side by side, both looking out at the slice of view. A large dark bird lifted itself up from the marsh and rose up through the sky.

"Look!" Clare said.

"It's the great blue heron," said Richard. "You can always tell, even at a distance, from the way it flaps its wings, slowly, like this." Richard rose up in his chair and moved his arms up and down. He looked, in profile, a bit like a heron himself. It had something to do with his distinctive nose, but it had mostly to do with his neck, which was long and thin, with a pronounced Adam's apple.

Richard's arms were graceful, and the way he dropped his wrists and let his fingers follow did look like the movement of the heron's wings. "Try it," Richard said.

Clare smiled.

"Come on," said Richard, "really try it." So Clare leaned forwards and moved her arms, too.

Richard sat back in his seat. "All right," he said. "Now back to business. What would you like to know about me?"

Clare rested her head back in her chair and closed her eyes. There were so many questions—it was hard to decide where to begin.

"What I want to know," she said, and she hesitated before she went on, "is whether you always were the way you are, or whether something happened, and made you change."

Richard let out a big breath of air. "That's a biggy, huh?"

Clare shrugged. "I guess."

"I think the answer is that sometimes people don't

really know themselves," said Richard. "I haven't changed, but it took me a long time to figure out who I was. For years I was afraid of finding out. It was a long, slow process. It began when I moved to Palo Alto."

"How come you got married, though?"

"That's what people did—what they still do, though now it's different," said Richard. "Besides, I was captivated by Vera—she had a vivid personality and she was beautiful." He laughed. "You're smiling Clare, but it's true. Vera was stunning. And she seemed so sure about me. It's a great thing, Clare, when you're not certain about yourself, to have someone else certain about you."

Clare opened her eyes and looked sideways at Richard. He was staring out at the marsh.

"I wasn't surprised when Vera's enthusiasm for me waned," he said. "When she became involved with Peter I wasn't surprised, either. I didn't expect her to come with me to California, and she didn't. Eventually I met other people. And then, slowly, things became clear to me." He turned to look at Clare.

"But that's not a reason for forgetting all about me," said Clare.

"I didn't forget about you, Clare."

"You might as well have."

"Oh no, Clare. That's not true. And I never forgot about you. I was trying to make your life easier by staying far away. I didn't want to be a problem for you."

"That's not a good excuse for staying away. You wouldn't have been a problem. Not to me!"

Richard was quiet for a moment, then he added, "Perhaps I was protecting myself, as well."

She let the words sit in her mind, and gradually her anger dissipated, until it was no longer there. She waited a moment more before speaking. "It's your turn to ask me a question now," she said.

"Is this hard for you?" he asked. "Finding this out?"

Clare shrugged. "A little," she said.

"I'm sorry about that," said Richard.

Clare looked down, then added, "But not nearly as hard as you seemed to think it would be."

Richard ran his hand along the wooden frame of his canvas chair. "I thought about not telling you," he said slowly. "But I couldn't see how I could have a relationship with you without you knowing. And it was important to me to establish a relationship with you. Charlie always wanted me to, and I put it off for much too long."

"Charlie knew about me?"

"He was my partner, Clare. We were together for six years. He knew everything about me."

"Were you going to get married?"

"We might have, but that possibility wasn't available in time for us."

Clare waited for a moment, then asked, "Was he sick for a long time?"

Richard seemed puzzled at first. Then he shook his head. "Charlie didn't die of AIDS, Clare. Is that what you were thinking?"

Clare nodded.

"Charlie was killed in an accident."

Clare felt so stupid she had to look away. She had missed what had been perfectly obvious. It was Charlie who had been hit by a car when he was on his bike. It was Charlie whom Richard had been thinking about that night when they were driving home from the pizza place.

Richard got up out of his seat. "How about we go

out and do some kayaking?" he asked. "Let's not do any netting of terrapins; let's just go out and paddle around, explore the bay."

"OK," said Clare.

Out on the water they didn't have to talk. They headed out into the bay. The sun glinted on the water and it looked as if the undersides of the waves were coated in silver. Clare's kayak nosed into the low waves and it felt good to be paddling hard into the wind, to put everything into her arms and hands. The spray was sharp and cold and pricked her sweating skin, but after she had been paddling for a while, she didn't feel it anymore.

19

Jaylin's family's boat was named *Breaking Point*, purchased, Jaylin explained, with money her father had gotten from his most recent book. While it seemed a reasonable title for a crime thriller, Clare thought it was an unfortunate choice for a boat. It was a white boat with a blue canvas awning and white, upholstered seats, and it looked brand new.

Clare had worn her swimsuit with a top that she found somewhat uncomfortable but which Susannah had told her "maximized her cleavage"—the little of it that there was. Richard had wanted to give her money to spend in town, but she'd said she didn't need it.

"I brought some with me," she said. "In fact it's the money you sent for my birthday."

"You mean you haven't spent it in all these months?" Richard asked.

"Uh uh."

"Vera lets you spend the money, doesn't she?" Richard asked.

"Oh, sure," said Clare. "It's me. I like to put it away to save up for something."

"Like what?"

"I don't know," said Clare. "I guess if I wanted to run away from home, I could buy a plane ticket somewhere. Once when Vera was being especially difficult I made a plan that I'd go out to California and look you up."

Richard didn't say anything for a moment. He took in his breath and let it out slowly. Finally he said, "You always would have been welcome, Clare. I don't know how we would have worked things out with Vera, but I would always have wanted to have you. But you had no way of knowing that, did you?"

"No," said Clare.

***

The tide was just beginning to rise so they waded out to the boat in shallow water and climbed up the swim ladder to get aboard. Kip reached out to help Clare step over the backseat and onto the deck, and she was so stunned by the fact that he had actually held her hand in his she forgot to say thank you until it was too late. She followed Jaylin up to the front of the boat and they settled on the wide seat that was built into the bow.

Kip helped Mark lug a cooler onto the boat and get the canvas covers stowed away in the compartments under the seats. Mark lowered the engine and started warming the motor.

"Aren't we waiting for your dad?" Clare asked.

"Oh, my dad's not coming. He's working on something."

"And your mom?" Clare asked.

"Mom? She won't step foot on a boat. She gets seasick just looking at one."

"Can Mark run the boat by himself?"

"Sure," said Jaylin. "Probably better than my dad. Dad's always getting new toys, but he never learns how to use them. He got a sailboat last year and took it out once and it capsized and we had to get the marine company to tow it back in."

Clare watched Mark who was sitting at the seat with all the dials. He did seem to know what he was doing. Still, when Richard, in deference to Vera, had asked her where she was going and with whom, she had said, "Jaylin's family," which had implied parents, hadn't it? Above all, she didn't want Richard to get into trouble with Vera.

Kip pulled up the swim ladder and then made his way to the front of the boat. He kneeled right next to Clare, so close the side of his leg pressed against hers. She leaned to the side so he could get access to the ropes and untie *Breaking Point* from the mooring.

"Can I help?" she asked.

"I'm good," he said.

His swim shorts pulled down a little on the side, exposing a half inch of not-yet-suntanned skin. If she touched him there she could cover the thin white crescent with her forefinger.

"All set?" Mark called.

"Ready to roll," said Kip, and he went back and

took the other seat in the center of the boat.

There was a pile of life jackets on the seats across from Jaylin and Clare, and Jaylin took two for them to use for backrests.

"Don't we have to put these on?" Clare asked.

"Only if you're going to be waterskiing or something," said Jaylin. "This boat is absolutely safe. It will float even if it hits an iceberg and gets a huge hole in its hull."

"I thought it was required to wear life jackets in boats," said Clare.

"Lord, you do worry about everything, don't you?" asked Jaylin.

"I don't know that I do, but my mother does," said Clare.

"Thank goodness she's not with us, then," said Jaylin. "Hey, have you ever been to P-Town before?" she asked.

Clare shook her head.

"Just wait! It's the wildest scene in the world. The streets are packed with the weirdest people you've ever seen. Last time there was a drag queen all in pink feathers. I'm not kidding you."

"Hey remember those guys in chaps with their hairy naked butts?" shouted Mark. Clare was surprised he had been able to hear their conversation over the noise of the engine.

"Don't scare her," said Jaylin to Mark. "That was at night," she said to Clare. "I don't think they parade around like that during the day."

Mark maneuvered *Breaking Point* out between the other boats moored on the side of the island. As soon as they were out in open water, he pulled the throttle way down and the boat took off, its bow rising up at such an angle that the life jackets flew off the seat and Clare gripped onto the railing to keep from sliding off. She didn't say a single word, but Jaylin saw the look on her face and said, "Don't worry, once we start planing we'll level off." They did level off, the boat rising high above the water so it seemed to be flying low over its surface. Each time they hit a wave, water sprayed up onto them. Clare was relieved when Jaylin suggested they sit on the seats that faced forwards. She got less wet, and she was able to brace her feet against the front seat.

Clare thought she had never been on anything so

fast in her life, not even Peter's motorcycle. In a few minutes they covered all the distance that had taken her and Richard nearly half an hour to do by kayak. She wasn't so frightened anymore now that the boat was more level. The bay seemed huge and glorious, and she felt a kind of exhilaration which she couldn't imagine she'd ever feel in a kayak. It seemed like a betrayal, though, of Richard. Richard, who saw speedboats as the enemies of his terrapins, who had contempt for the kind of people who owned them.

Clare leaned around to look at the view behind her. Blackfish Island was in the distance, growing smaller and smaller, by the second. Soon the big houses, like Jaylin's, along the top of the dunes grew indistinct, and the island itself melted into a low, dark shape. Suddenly the wind caught the edge of Clare's visor. She couldn't grab it in time, and it flew off her head and in a second it was gone. Jaylin shouted to Mark to stop the boat. He cut the engine.

"You want me to go back for a stupid visor?" he asked.

"It's OK," said Clare. "It's not like it's that valuable or anything."

"I see it," said Jaylin, pointing. "It's floating right there."

"I thought we were going to Provincetown," said Mark.

"Come on, Mark," said Kip. "Give her a break. Circle around and I'll grab it with the boat hook." Mark reluctantly turned the boat around and after three passes Kip was able to snag the waterlogged visor and bring it on board. He held it out to Clare. It was a dripping, white thing.

"Catch of the day," he said.

Clare lifted the sodden visor from the hook. The proper response would have been to say something about a gallant knight, but that was too big a risk. It was simpler to just say, "Thank you." And then, to show that she was a good sport, she squeezed out some of the water and put the visor back on her head. "It's a lot cooler this way," she said.

Jaylin smiled appreciatively, and looked over at Mark and gave a little nod to show her approval—a communication between siblings.

They crossed the protected inner bay and reached the sandy strip of land coming out from the mainland which separated the harbor from the open water of Cape Cod Bay. Mark chose to cross over in a shallow channel rather than go all the way to the end, the long way around.

"You're supposed to go around the point," said Jaylin. "It's too shallow here."

"What do you know?" asked Mark.

"I can read the chart."

"Well, good for you," said Mark.

"Go ahead, then," said Jaylin, "and when you wreck the boat you can't say I didn't warn you. And I've got witnesses to prove it. Right, Clare?"

Clare didn't know what to say, so she just nodded.

"Right, Kip?" asked Jaylin.

Kip held up his hands. "Hey, I'm staying out of this," he said.

Mark raised the engine halfway, and then steered the boat over the sandbar. Clare thought it looked like it was only a foot deep, but surely it had to be deeper than that. On the open bay side there was a wind, and at this spot, where the tide was coming up, there were large, black waves. The boat bucked and shook, and the bow rose so high it seemed the boat would flip over, then came crashing down. Waves broke over the bow. Clare clutched the metal rail. Even Jaylin looked frightened.

When they made it through the rough patch of water and then leveled off, Mark, exuberant, gave a whoop. Clare thought he had probably been frightened, too. "Hey, that was fun," he said. "Let's try it again!"

"Don't be an asshole," said Jaylin.

"I thought you wanted to get to P-Town," said Kip, and Clare looked at him with gratitude.

Mark either gave in, or he was just kidding. He grabbed a can of beer from the cooler and tossed one to Kip. Jaylin didn't saying anything about them drinking beer. "Hand us some sodas," she said.

"Get them yourself," said Mark. Jaylin dug out two sodas and handed one to Clare. The last thing Clare wanted was a stomach full of soda, but she took it from Jaylin's hand. She didn't have to drink it.

Mark, emboldened by his success with the channel, and perhaps by the beer as well, drove the boat fast and wildly all the way to Provincetown, every so often circling back so they would go through their own wake. Mark and Kip had another beer each, and soon Kip was whooping with Mark each time they slammed through the waves.

Each time, Clare clutched the metal railing and prayed they'd get through all right. By the time they got to Provincetown she was nauseated and the muscle in her hand ached.

From the waterside, Provincetown looked like a seaside village in a stage set. They came in around a jetty and Mark managed, somehow, to navigate among the other boats and pull in close to the town landing. It took him several tries before he was able to get the boat anchored.

Clare had brought a plastic bag to carry her things, as Jaylin had advised, and she lowered herself carefully down the swim ladder and held the bag on her head as she waded to shore. There was a small public beach area, where Clare pulled shorts and a shirt on over her bathing suit, and just beyond was Commercial Street, so jammed with pedestrians that the few cars that dared to drive along it could barely get through.

"Let's go get some lunch," said Jaylin.

"Sounds good," said Mark.

It was strange walking along wearing aqua shoes. They made squelching noises with each step. As they made their way along Commercial Street Jaylin darted into shops to look at clothes. She didn't seem concerned that her feet were wet, even in stores where the clothing was so expensive even Vera wouldn't shop there. The street was a carnival with packs of gawking tourists. There were more outlandish getups than Clare had ever seen, and one drag queen with a platinum blonde wig.

Mark and Kip were walking ahead, with Clare and Jaylin just behind, when they passed close by two perfectly ordinary men, who were holding hands. Not quite out of earshot, Mark turned back to Jaylin and said, "Ew! Did you see those fags?"

Fags. The word struck Clare as if it were an actual object someone had thrown at her, not just a sound in the air. It was a word that her friends would never use, and in the past she would have been startled if she heard someone say it. But now it was different. It wasn't just an offending word; it was about her father. It was about her. Everything was different now.

Mark held his hands out, like a limp ballerina,

and wriggled his rear end. He laughed out loud and bumped his hip against Kip's. Kip laughed, too, and swiveled his hips. They turned around for Jaylin and Clare's benefit. Jaylin joined them laughing.

Clare didn't laugh, but she didn't say anything either. The whole thing made her feel sick. It wasn't just Mark making fun of the men—it was Kip, too. Kip whom she had liked so much—and it was Jaylin laughing with them. But it was more than what they were doing. It was that she didn't have the courage to say anything about it.

The restaurant they went to for lunch overlooked the harbor, but even the view of the glimmering water and the boats bobbing pleasantly didn't get the image out of Clare's head of those two men and Mark's mocking them.

"If you keep your menu open like that," said Jaylin, "the waiter won't know we're ready to order."

Clare had been holding her menu without really looking at it. She glanced at it quickly. The sandwiches all had names, and the cheapest one was ten dollars. She didn't feel like eating anything, but Jaylin was looking at her impatiently, so she ordered the Shank

Painter Pita. When the waiter had turned his back on them, Mark waggled his fingers in the air and he and Kip collapsed against each other, laughing. Clare watched the waiter as he headed off towards the back of the restaurant and pushed through the swinging door to the kitchen. He was a thin young man, but there wasn't anything particular about him that made him identifiable as gay. What was it that made Mark think he was? Would he think that Richard was gay just by looking at him? Clare looked down at the pine table. It was varnished so thickly she could dig her fingernail into the shine and leave a nick. When she looked up again Mark was staring at her.

"Hey, what's up with you?" he asked.

"Nothing," said Clare.

"You look kind of out of it," said Mark.

"I guess that's just the way I look," said Clare. She wanted to tell him what she thought of the way they were acting. But what was the point of it? She wasn't going to be able to change them. Yet that wasn't the real reason she didn't speak up; the real reason was that, somehow, she couldn't. She just wanted to hide under the table.

"You don't look as if you're having a very good time," said Jaylin. "You're in P-town. You're supposed to be having a good time."

The door to the kitchen swung open again and Clare saw the waiter coming out with a tray with drinks on it. She was afraid it was for them. She got up quickly from the table and told Jaylin she was going to the ladies' room. She didn't want to be at the table when the waiter came over to them. She didn't want to be around in case Mark and Kip did anything. She didn't want to be around them at all.

The bathroom had pink ceramic tile and a pink ruffled curtain at the window, but there was no glass in the window, just an air conditioner, so Clare couldn't look outside. On the wall there were two rusty metal dispensers, one for pads and tampons and the other for perfume. There were five choices of perfumes with names like Secrecy and Midnight in Paris. Clare didn't have a quarter, but she pushed each of the plungers. Nothing came out. There were two toilet stalls and when women came in to use the bathroom Clare pretended she was combing her hair.

Eventually Jaylin came to see if she was all right.

"We're practically finished eating," she said. "What's the matter with you?"

"I just don't feel great," said Clare. "I think I got too much sun and I got a little seasick coming over."

"That's too bad," said Jaylin. "We're going to have to leave pretty soon because the tide is starting to go out."

Clare caught a glimpse of her face in the mirror, right over the sign that said *Employees Must Wash their Hands*. She did look sunburned.

"Actually," she said, "I won't be going back with you." She hadn't planned on saying this, but it popped right out.

"What do you mean?" asked Jaylin.

"I'm really sorry," said Clare, "but I just don't feel like being on a boat."

"So how are you going to get back, then?" asked Jaylin.

"I'm going to get my dad to come pick me up," said Clare. She was amazed at her own audacity. Seeing Jaylin's surprised face she added, "You're welcome to drive back with me."

"Why would I want to do that?" asked Jaylin.

Clare shrugged.

20

Jaylin waved once at Clare and called out, "See you!" as she, Mark, and Kip headed off back down Commercial Street to the town landing. But Clare doubted they would be seeing each other again. She hadn't brought her cell phone with her, since they were traveling in an open boat, but she'd seen public telephones near the wharf. As she walked there, she felt less brave, less certain, and by the time she reached the phones, she was beginning to feel terrified. What if she couldn't get in touch with Richard? Or what if he wasn't able to come?

Richard didn't answer the phone. His answering machine picked up after the sixth ring and informed her of the number of the terrapin hotline to report sightings, then clicked right off. She called back again to try to leave a message, but the answering machine cut off immediately after the recording, and she was speaking to a dial tone. It had been reassuring, for a moment, to hear his voice.

Every ten minutes she tried calling him again, hanging up just before the answering machine picked up since she didn't have much change left. Richard wasn't expecting her home till late in the afternoon, so there was no reason he should be around the house. He could be on the beach or out in his kayak or even on the other side of the Blackfish Island Bridge. She tried picturing him in different places, as if that was a way to make him real, summon him home. But the scene that she kept returning to in her mind was when Richard had demonstrated how to get back into a kayak after it capsized and he'd been trying to hoist himself up; his hair and beard were soaking wet and his legs were thrashing in the water.

In between calls, Clare took short walks onto the wharf. The ferry from Boston had recently arrived, and an onslaught of people—pulling suitcases and carrying satchels—approached Clare. There were gay couples and straight couples and people on their own who might have been gay or straight. Here, it didn't seem to matter. Some of the people looked dazed, as if they had been deposited in a foreign country, but some of them had been met by friends or family and Clare looked with envy at these small scenes of happy reconnection. Soon they were all gone, absorbed into the life of Provincetown. The whale-watch boats were all out for the day, and for a time, the wharf was quiet.

Clare tried to think about what else she could do. There was no public transportation to Blackfish Island. There might be taxis somewhere, but she hadn't seen any. She didn't know anyone in Provincetown, though; she didn't know anyone on the Cape. There was that woman, Steffi, but she didn't even know her last name. She could call Aunt Eva, but she'd only get her worried. It wasn't as if Eva could just drive down from Maine and pick her up. There really wasn't anyone else to call except Richard. Eventually he'd have to come home.

At last Richard answered the phone. He sounded breathless at first, as if he had run to catch the call. "I'll be there as soon as I can," he said. He didn't sound either angry or surprised. He didn't ask her any questions, either.

Half an hour later, when Clare saw his old station wagon inching its way through traffic towards the wharf, she ran towards it. It was the same car that she had felt so uncomfortable riding in when she had first been picked up by Richard at the Cape Cod Canal, and now it was the most welcome sight in the world.

Richard spotted her and stopped so she could jump into the car. "Are you all right?" he asked once she was settled in her seat.

"I'm fine," said Clare. "I just didn't want to have to go back with them on the boat."

"Where are they?" asked Richard, looking out the window.

"They left a while ago."

Richard stepped on the brake and turned to look at Clare.

"That man should be shot," said Richard.

"Who?"

"Your friend's father—leaving you alone before I arrived to pick you up."

Then Clare had to explain how it had turned out

that Jaylin's father didn't go with them at all; it was just Jaylin and her brother and his friend. And the reason they had to leave was because of the tide. She sounded as if she were defending them, and she wasn't sure why.

Richard didn't say anything.

It was a relief to get out through the crowded streets of Provincetown and out into the open highway. Clare rolled her window all the way down and let the warm highway wind blow against her face.

She looked over at Richard. "How come you're not asking me why I didn't go back with them?" she asked.

"I figured if you wanted me to know, you'd tell me," said Richard.

"I wouldn't have gone with them in the first place if I'd known Jaylin's father wasn't coming, but I was already on the boat and they'd started it up."

"It's all right, Clare. I understand."

"How come you're being so nice?" asked Clare.

"Why shouldn't I be?"

"I made you come all the way to Provincetown to get me."

"That's nothing," said Richard.

The car wheels thumped a welcoming drumbeat

on the planks of the Blackfish Island Bridge. Clare took in a deep breath of the reassuring smell of the marsh. She felt as if she was coming home. Everything was distorted in Provincetown. Now, on Blackfish Island, everything was restored. Richard, here, was just a man who studied terrapins.

"The reason I didn't want to go back with them is that I got a little scared on the boat," said Clare. "Jaylin's brother likes going through the waves." Clare paused for a moment, then added, "And he and his friend were kind of obnoxious."

"And your friend Jaylin?"

Clare didn't say anything.

"Not such a good friend?"

"Not really," said Clare, softly.

"I'm sorry I was out walking on the beach. You were trying to get me on the phone for a long time, weren't you?" asked Richard.

"Yes."

"And she left before she knew you had been able to get a ride?"

Clare nodded. She hadn't thought she was going to cry, but she was crying now, silly, burbling kind of crying, like a little kid. She'd told Richard only part of the reason, but somehow she thought that maybe he guessed. He seemed always to figure things out.

"Oh, Sweetie," said Richard. He took the steering wheel in his left hand and with his right hand he reached out towards Clare and stroked her hair back over her head. His hand rested there behind her head and she leaned back into it, and let the weight of her head, the weight of everything, rest in his palm.

21

They went out together early in the morning to check for terrapin tracks. It was almost the end of the nesting season, and Richard said no new nests had been found for the past two days.

"We get a break until the end of August," said Richard. "Then we have to check all the marked sites every day to see if any hatchlings have emerged."

"I wish I could be here to help," said Clare.

"Maybe you could come back then," said Richard. "If Vera will let you."

"She'll have to let me," said Clare.

It was a foggy morning. Richard was wearing his usual clothes—tan shorts and blue work shirt—but

Clare was glad she had grabbed her sweatshirt when they left the house. The sky and the water were the same almost colorless grey-blue, and there was no horizon. Even the big houses on the top of the dunes were softened, some of their extremities lost in the mist. Some black-backed gulls strutted along the flats. One found a spider crab worth eating and took it off to devour on an upturned dingy, but a more aggressive gull snatched it away. The loser's complaint was the only sound on the entire beach.

They walked almost halfway around the island, and didn't spot any terrapin tracks.

"This could be it," said Richard, "but I'll keep looking. There are sometimes a few late nesters."

"What are you going to do with your mornings if you're not out checking for terrapin tracks?" asked Clare.

"Oh, I'm sure I'll find something," said Richard. "There's always mountains of data to study."

Slowly clouds in the sky began to take on definition and now and then the sun managed to push its way through and brighten patches of the beach. Clare took off her sweatshirt and tied it around her waist.

"Why do you care about them so much?" asked Clare.

"Do you think I care about them too much?"

"I'm not saying it's too much," said Clare. "It's just that I wondered why them? And why you?"

"Want to sit down for a minute? Take a break?" asked Richard.

"Sure," said Clare.

They walked up towards the dunes, where the sand was drier, and sat down next to each other. Vera would never sit on bare sand, only on a beach chair or a blanket. Clare was thinking about how she had changed since she first came to the island, when she, like Vera, would have always had something between herself and the beach.

"When Charlie died," began Richard, "I felt I had no one; I had nothing. I couldn't think of what to do with myself. I'd made enough money so I didn't have to work anymore, and there wasn't anything keeping me in California. So I came back here."

Richard picked up a handful of sand and then opened his fingers just enough so it flowed out, like a sand timer, depositing a small, even mound of sand.

"I'd never been particularly interested in nature before I met Charlie," he continued, "but he was a science teacher and loved all those creepy, crawly things, and eventually he won me over." Richard paused and looked directly at Clare. "I couldn't save Charlie," he said. "The terrapins were here. I thought I stood a fighting chance of saving some of them."

"What do you mean you couldn't save Charlie?" asked Clare.

"I was right there when he was hit," said Richard. "I was coiling up the hose by the garage door. Charlie had just come home and was picking up the mail from the box at the end of the driveway. I looked up when I heard him push the metal mailbox closed. He was straddling his bike, flipping through the mail. I saw the car coming fast around the curve in the road. I couldn't get to him in time."

Richard rested his elbows on his knees and sunk his face against the heels of his hands. His voice was muffled. "Dear God," he said, "why am I telling you all this?"

Clare looked out at the wide, flat beach. The water was gone, returned to the bay, but you could tell how far it had risen towards the dunes, and you could read the pattern of its movements in the ripples it had left behind.

Clare looked back at Richard. Their arms were almost touching and she leaned sideways and tilted her head so she was leaning against his shoulder.

"You do have someone," she whispered. "You have me."

Richard put his arm around her and pulled her close to him, so her cheek was against his collarbone. He didn't cry so you could hear him, but she could feel him crying. She slipped her arms around him and pressed her face against his chest.

22

The clouds covered the sun and once again it turned cool. When the rain started, Richard told Clare to go back the way they'd come, the shorter way home. He'd continue to circle the longer way around the island, checking for terrapin tracks, and meet her back at the house.

Clare pulled the hood of her sweatshirt over her head and pulled the sleeves down over her hands. She jogged a distance and then, when she was tired, she walked.

She wasn't looking for terrapin tracks, but her eyes, once trained to search for them, spotted them instinctively. They were fresh tracks, she could tell, and they were headed up from the water, towards the dunes. While she and Richard had been sitting together down the beach, a terrapin had come up on the shore and walked right across the footprints that Clare and Richard had left in the sand. Clare looked down the beach to where she had parted with Richard, but he had already gone around the corner of the island, and she couldn't see him. She followed the tracks up across the beach, lost them in the softer sand of the low dunes, and picked them up again. The beach grass pricked her ankles.

She saw the terrapin before she heard her, and Clare instantly dropped into a crouch. The terrapin must have just buried her newly laid eggs, and now she was tamping the sand down on the spot with her plastron, her bottom shell. She smoothed the sand and disguised the spot so that it would look like any other place in the dunes. She moved professionally and quickly, so intent on her business that Clare wasn't sure if she hadn't been seen, or if she had been, but was just ignored. When the terrapin turned to start walking back to the water Clare spotted the mark on her shell. It was Eleanor. It had to be. Clare had an urge to call out to her, to make a connection, but she knew the best thing for her to do was to keep still. She stayed low and watched Eleanor, who, at last satisfied, scrambled over the beach grass, down through the dunes. Clare stood up now to watch her. She moved faster than Clare ever thought a turtle could move, across the stretch of open beach and back down into the water. She never once looked back at the nesting spot she had made, to the future generation of terrapins she had left, as a promise, behind.

It was raining heavier now, and Clare knew the tracks might soon be lost. She studied the spot to memorize it, found a piece of driftwood to mark the place, and piled a cairn of stones at the edge of the dune where the nest was made. Then she started running to get Richard. He was a fast walker, and she calculated that she'd catch him sooner if she met him as he came around the island on the other side.

She started running, but she didn't run very far before she tired out. She cut across the dunes and took the dirt road through the center of the island, near their house, and then cut down to the marsh. She hiked along the mat of reeds at the high-tide line. In the distance she finally saw Richard, walking in her direction. She broke into a run.

"Daddy!" she cried. "Daddy! Daddy!" The word had come to her from someplace deep inside her; it came unbidden, like a snatch of music you didn't remember you'd ever heard. He wasn't Richard, or Dad. He was Daddy. It was his name in the language of her childhood, the name she had called him once, so long ago that she hadn't remembered. It was the name from when she had been that little girl in the photograph. It had been here, waiting for her on Blackfish Island, just as he had been here waiting for her, too.

ACKNOWLEDGMENTS

With gratitude to my editor, Andrew Karre, well met on "Blackfish Island"; my agent, Edward Necarsulmer IV; my writing group: Barbara Diamond Goldin, Patricia MacLachlan, Lesléa Newman, Ann Turner, Ellen Wittlinger, and Jane Yolen; Elaine Lasker von Bruns; Artemis Demas Roehrig; and, as always, Matthew Roehrig.

Special thanks to diamondback terrapin experts: Barbara Brennessel, Don Lewis, and Bob Prescott, and to Mass Audubon's Wellfleet Bay Wildlife Sanctuary.

ABOUT THE AUTHOR

Corinne Demas is the award-winning author of numerous books for children and adults, including *Everything I Was* for Carolrhoda Lab and *The Writing Circle*. She is Professor of English at Mount Holyoke College and a fiction editor of *The Massachusetts Review*. She lives with her family, her dog, and two miniature donkeys in Western Massachusetts and spends the summer on Cape Cod. Visit her online at www.corinnedemas.com.